Confessions of a Class Clown

Also by Arianne Costner

My Life as a Potato

Confessions of a Class Clown

ARIANNE COSTNER

Illustrations by Billy Yong

A YEARLING BOOK

Text copyright © 2022 by Arianne Costner
Cover art copyright © 2022 by Alex Jefferies
Interior illustrations copyright © 2022 by Billy Yong

All rights reserved. Published in the United States by Yearling, an imprint of Random House Children's Books, a division of Penguin Random House LLC, New York. Originally published in hardcover in the United States by Random House Children's Books, a division of Penguin Random House LLC, New York, in 2022.

Yearling and the jumping horse design are registered trademarks of Penguin Random House LLC.

Visit us on the Web! rhcbooks.com

Educators and librarians, for a variety of teaching tools, visit us at RHTeachersLibrarians.com

The Library of Congress has cataloged the hardcover edition of this work as follows:
Name: Costner, Arianne, author.
Title: Confessions of a class clown / Arianne Costner.
Description: First edition. | New York: Random House Children's Books, [2021]
Summary: Seventh grader Jack Reynolds loves making people laugh but he needs help to make his wacky MyTube channel take off, and making friends is not exactly his strong suit.
Identifiers: LCCN 2020025247 | ISBN 978-0-593-11870-2 (hardcover) |
ISBN 978-0-593-11871-9 (lib. bdg.) | ISBN 978-0-593-11872-6 (ebook)
Subjects: CYAC: Friendship—Fiction. | Conduct of life—Fiction. | Middle schools—Fiction. | Schools—Fiction. | Internet videos—Fiction. | Humorous stories.
Classification: LCC PZ7.1.C6747 Con 2021 | DDC [Fic]—dc23

ISBN 978-0-593-11873-3 (paperback)

Printed in the United States of America
10 9 8 7 6 5 4 3 2 1
First Yearling Edition 2023

To Kevin, for helping me discover this story

Contents

1

Just Trying to Keep Things Interesting

T-rexing is an art understood by many yet mastered by few.

It starts with the squat. Most people skip this important step. To convincingly play a T. rex, you gotta crouch a little, with your legs spread apart, and lean forward on your toes.

Then there's the arm perch. Pretend your upper arms are superglued nice and tight to the sides of your torso. If you've got your elbows flopping all over, you've ruined the moment.

Finally, there's the highlight of T-rexing: the roar. The ideal sound is something like half hawk, half elephant. The more obnoxious the better. Oh, and raise the back of the roof of your mouth for volume. That's a trick I learned last fall in beginners' choir before I got kicked out. (I sang too loud, apparently. Proof the trick works.)

You might be asking yourself, "Who is this rare genius speaking to me? And how has he mastered the art of T-rexing at such a young age?"

Nice to meet you. I'm Jack Reynolds. Making a fool of myself is my life's work. I figure that in middle school, you're gonna look like a doofus anyway. You might as well own it.

I burst into first-period English wearing green checkered socks and my hoodie strings scrunched tight, so my nose peeps out of a small clothy circle.

"GRAWUUUREEEEAAAARRR!" I perch my arms at my sides and wiggle them around. It's not my best roar—a little heavy on the hawk—but it does the trick. Most people smile, some laugh, and some roll their eyes. But most smile, and that's the important part.

I can't claim I *invented* T-rexing, but I'm the one who

made it popular here at Franklin Middle School. I've made lots of things popular. Marshmallow sniping. Bubble Wrap scarves. I have to say, though, that T-rexing is my crowning achievement. Just two weeks ago, I posted a video of me T-rexing through a JOANN Fabrics store, and it already has over four thousand views on MyTube. (MyTube, by the way, is basically the world's greatest app. It's like if YouTube and Instagram had a better-looking child.)

"Jack." Ms. Campbell looks a little like a candy cane this morning in her red-and-white-striped shirt. She presses her honey-colored bangs against her forehead like she usually does when she's frustrated. "How many times have I told you? No dinosaur noises in class."

"You said no T. rex noises." I flap my arms. "That was clearly a Pteranodon."

Ms. Campbell keeps a straight face, but a smile cracks in the corners of her eyes. "At least you're early. Get to your seat before the bell."

You wouldn't know it, but Ms. Campbell is my favorite teacher. She's about my mom's age and has this cool gap between her two front teeth. She lets us act out scenes from books, and makes funny voices when she reads. Listening to her read is probably the only thing I like about school.

I loosen my hoodie strings and head to my seat. It waits for me in the back row, far left, aka the most boring corner of the room. Ms. Campbell has surrounded me with some of the best-behaved kids in the class like she's using them as a fort of protection to separate me from my innocent class-mates.

It's not a bad strategy.

Ever since first grade, I've been what you'd call a class clown. I don't mind the label. I wear it well. Six-year-old me couldn't spell or hold scissors right, but I could glue foam pieces to my nose and run around.

Everyone's gotta be good at something, right?

I take a detour on the way to my seat to pass by Zane's desk, three rows over. He and I have been pretty tight ever since he randomly invited me to go laser tagging with him and his friends a few weeks ago. Before that, we'd just mess around in class, chucking erasers at each other and stuff. It's been fun to start hanging out with him outside of school.

Zane's the kind of guy who everyone knows, even if he's never talked to you a day in your life. For the past three years, he's thrown a huge back-to-school pool party at his house, complete with water guns and chocolate fountains and the newest Marvel movie playing on a projector screen. He's running for class president, and he's a shoo-in to win. Especially with the Pokémon-themed posters I helped him design.

You wouldn't think Zane and I have much in common. For one, he's a football guy—or was last semester, during football season. Me? I'm about as athletic as a stick of string cheese, although I was pretty good at T-ball as a kid. (It's not fair how that stops being impressive after you turn seven.) Zane and I also have different styles. I wear cartoon shirts and Converse. He wears jerseys and training pants (which is another word for sweatpants, but I like saying training pants because it sounds like a diaper). He goes skiing every other weekend, while I've somehow managed to live in Utah for the past thirteen years without ever hitting the slopes. The main thing we both like is making MyTube videos. In fact, he was the one who recorded my first T-rexing. It was his idea to do it in JOANN's, because if they banned us from the store—which they did—we wouldn't care.

I slap his desk. "'Sup, coolio?"

He glances up. "Oh, hey."

That's weird. He's supposed to say, *'Sup, broski.* It's tradition.

There's an awkward silence, so I grab his pencil and start twirling it.

He straightens his back and shakes his hair out of his eyes. "Hey, don't lose that. It's my only pencil."

I pinch the pencil like a dart. "Think I could get it to stick in the ceiling?"

"Don't." He snatches it out of my hand. Geesh. *Someone's* having a bad day.

"I was just kidding," I mumble.

"Hey, Zane," Jared Pearson says as he walks into class. Jared's a big dude. Like, probably the size I would be if I ate steak every night and was the literal son of Thor. He lifts his chin. "Ready to get gains later?"

"'Gains'?" I say. "What's that?"

Zane twirls his pencil, which is pretty hypocritical, since he just got mad at me for doing the exact same thing. "It means we're lifting. I didn't think you'd be interested."

Lifting weights? We're in seventh grade. We're supposed to be worried about homework and body odor. Since when are we supposed to work out?

Still, I'm annoyed I wasn't invited to get these "gains," as uninteresting as it sounds.

I flex my nonexistent muscles. "You don't think these babies can take a challenge?"

The girl in front of us giggles, but Zane doesn't.

"Five seconds to the bell!" calls Ms. Campbell. For once, I'm glad class is about to start. I make a show of running through the aisles and plopping my butt into my chair right as the bell rings.

Ms. Campbell hushes the class and holds up a stack of papers. "Who can run this down to room twelve?"

I wave my hands wildly, but she ignores me and picks Brielle instead. No shocker there. Brielle Kimball is this perfect girl who gets tons of awards and dots the *i*'s in her name with little hearts. That's the type that always gets picked to run errands for the teacher. I'm perfectly capable of transporting papers down a hallway, but teachers won't give me the chance.

After Brielle leaves, Ms. Campbell passes worksheets down the aisles, and lots of us moan. "It's a fascinating passage," she says. "I promise."

Looking over the worksheet makes my brain shrivel three sizes. There's a reading passage about owl pellets, followed by five multiple-choice questions. I always get the answers wrong, so what's the point? I write my name in big block letters at the top of the paper: *J-A-C-K*. Then I skip the passage, guess *D, A, B, B, B* as the answers, and doodle a T. rex in the margin. He's eating marshmallows and growling because they keep getting stuck in his pointy teeth. His tiny arms can't even reach up to pick them out. Man, it would stink to be a T. rex.

The intercom crackles, and one of the eighth-grade student council members begins the morning announcements. *"Good morning, Franklin Middle School!"* she chirps as Ms. Campbell scrawls the daily agenda on the board with her fading blue marker.

"We hope you're getting your acts ready for the talent show. Tryouts are next Thursday, so come prepared!"

Zane and I have this awesomesauce evil plan for the talent show. We'll try out with a normal act—like singing (despite getting kicked out of choir, I'm not bad)—and then do

7

something totally unexpected for the actual performance. Something that'll make us go viral. We haven't figured it out yet, but I think it's gonna incorporate cheese balls.

I point at Zane and sing in a nasally pop-star voice, *"Are you reeeeady?"* He doesn't even turn his head. Maybe he didn't know that was directed at him.

"Wait, are you guys doing something for the talent show?" says Karlie, who sits on the outer edge of my quiet-kid fort.

"You bet we are," I say.

"Ha! Maybe I'll actually go," says the guy sitting next to her.

At least *they* seem excited about our act. I hope Zane realizes that people are expecting big things from us.

At the other end of the classroom, Zane chucks an eraser at Jared's back. That's *our* thing!

I scowl and draw my T. rex longer arms to show him a little mercy.

"And after school, make sure to check out our new speed-friendshipping program in the drama room," says the announcement girl. *"Come to sit, chat, and relax. You might even meet your new bestie!"*

I scoff. Meet your new bestie? She makes it sound so easy. You can't just pick up a bestie after talking to them for a few minutes. Trust me, I would know.

Why is it that in movies, kids always have this super-tight friend group that they hang out with all the time? They have their lunch spots and secret handshakes and cheesy stuff like that. Real life isn't that way.

Or maybe it is for everyone except me.

I look at Zane. I can't say he's my *best* friend. We've hung out a few times and sit together most days in the cafeteria, so I thought we were heading in that direction. But now he's being weird. He tosses another eraser at Jared's back, and I can hear our friendship fizzling out like a cheap sparkler on the Fourth of July. *Fzzzzzz.*

There are a couple of other guys I used to hang out with, and things ended the same way. Tyrone, who got super into band and never had time. Derek, who got all googly-eyed with his girlfriend and stopped wanting to talk to anyone else. I still say hi to those guys in the halls—it's not like we're frenemies (a word I can't believe I just used)—but it feels like I got ditched, and I have no idea why. With Zane, I thought things might be different. I mean, two weeks ago on April Fool's, we were Saran-wrapping all the school toilets. If that's not a sign of true friendship, I don't know what is.

Ms. Campbell's almost done writing on the board. Her red-and-white shirt starts to look less like a candy cane and more like a bull's-eye.

I've got it.

Zane just needs to remember why we became friends in the first place. If there's one thing I know about him, it's that he can't resist a good prank.

And I have just the thing.

2

~~Don't~~ Try This at Home, Kids

I reach into my pocket and pull out a mini marshmallow. Why is there a mini marshmallow in my pocket, you ask? Because my name is Jack Reynolds. If I don't have a sandwich bag filled with mini marshmallows at all times, then who even am I?

Marshmallow sniping is not my most popular trend, but it's definitely my most delicious. The idea's simple enough. You roll a piece of construction paper into a tube, stick a marshmallow inside, and blow it at an unsuspecting victim. Ninety percent of the time, they don't feel it. The challenge is to see how many times you can snipe someone before they notice the floor around them is covered with little white puffies.

This was supposed to be my splashy debut at the start of the school year, but it never caught on. Most kids are on their best behavior during the first couple of weeks, so that was bad planning on my part. A small group of us got into it, but it got banned once the teachers noticed marshmallows sticking to the bottom of everyone's shoes.

I still carry marshmallows around, though. I need my daily fix of the melt-in-your-mouth goodness. They're part of my brand. Mom refuses to buy them, so I save up spare change and get them at the corner gas station. I could be addicted to worse things.

I scan my desk for blow-dart materials. A file folder would be ideal, but all I have is my old green notebook.

I tear the cover off, gently separating the cardboard from the binder rings. It makes a *zzzrip* sound that Ms. Campbell probably would've noticed if she hadn't banished me to the back corner, so joke's on her.

"All right," Ms. Campbell says once the announcements end. She displays the cover of a tattered-looking book. "We're going to start reading one of my favorite novels. *The Outsiders*."

She talks up the book for a bit. Something about social cliques and greasy kids. Under my desk, I roll the notebook cover into a thin tube.

"The story takes place in the 1960s," Ms. Campbell continues. "Before I was born, if you can believe it! Back when

T. rexes roamed the earth." A few pity laughs follow. "We'll get to learn lots of interesting information about this time period. Let's make a *K-W-L* chart."

We make this chart at the beginning of every book we read. Ms. Campbell tosses her old blue marker into the trash and switches to red. She writes "The 1960s" in big swoopy letters and then makes three columns underneath. The *K* column is where she writes stuff we already know. The *W* column is for stuff we want to know. And the *L* column is for stuff we learn as we study.

"All right. First column. What do we know about the 1960s?"

The room responds with silence and blank stares. Too bad Ms. Campbell sent Brielle to deliver papers. She's the main commenter.

After several seconds, "Get Gains" Jared raises his hand. "Weren't there, like, hippies?"

People laugh, including Zane. It wasn't even that funny.

Ms. Campbell uncaps her marker. "That's right." While she writes "Hippies" under the *K* column, I stuff a marshmallow into the blow tube, bring it to my mouth, and puff soft and quick, like I'm blowing out a candle. The marshmallow flings across the room but lands short in the middle of an aisle. I think only the quiet-fort kids notice, but they don't react. I'll have to do better.

Someone else raises their hand, and I repeat the process.

This time the marshmallow lands about a yard away from Ms. Campbell's feet. Several people turn to face me, their eyes bugging out like they're goldfish. I put my finger to my lips and wink.

People are catching on, and my audience is growing. I make eye contact with Zane, point to my phone, and mouth "record." He cringes a little, but the kids around him smile and nod, so he pulls out his phone.

Bada-bing, bada-boom. Things are starting to feel normal again.

Ms. Campbell faces forward. "What else do we know about the 1960s?"

Four hands shoot up. Ms. Campbell is visibly pleased. "There were hippie vans," one girl says.

"That would go under the hippie section. Let's think of an answer that doesn't involve hippies."

"They had tie-dyed shirts?" says a guy in the front row. Ms. Campbell sighs and turns to write.

His answer was short, so I barely have time to set my target. When I puff, the marshmallow detours and hits the wall to my right. Audible groans rumble across the room.

"Fish sticks!" I whisper. I've been trying to get the expression *fish sticks* to catch on, just to see if I can.

"Is something wrong?" Ms. Campbell twists around, and Zane stuffs his phone between his thighs.

No one dares make a peep. Finally, this girl named

Devyn casually says, "No." Major respect to her. I'll have to remember to fist-bump her after class.

Ms. Campbell scrunches her lips. "Okaaay," she says slowly. "Let's move to the *W* column. What's something you'd like to learn about the 1960s?"

I raise my hand. I have to give an extra-long answer so she'll face the board long enough for me to prepare my aim. All I know about the 1960s is that people didn't have cell phones, so I go with that. "I wanna know how they survived without having smartphones or the internet. Like, how did they know stuff, or talk to anyone, or *not* die from boredom?"

"Jack, that is a wonderful question, and I'm sure we can really delve into some deep answers. Let's see . . . how can I phrase this?" She turns around and I nod at Zane. He lifts his phone and shoots me a finger gun. I whip out my blow dart and take a deep breath. This is my last shot. Ms. Campbell's onto us, and the class will start to lose interest if I keep missing my target.

One-two-three-PUFF!

The marshmallow soars on a straight track toward the board. I can feel it in my skinny little bones. This is it.

The marshmallow lands smack-dab in the middle of Ms. Campbell's hair and—you wouldn't believe it—sticks! Ca-*ching*! This video's gonna blow up.

The class can't handle it. Who could blame them? A few people burst out laughing, and even the quiet girl next to me covers her mouth and gasps.

Ah, man. I live for this stuff.

"That's it." Ms. Campbell snaps around so sharply that the marshmallow in her hair bounces to the floor. "What. Is. Going. *On?*"

The room falls silent like somebody pressed the Mute button. I smoosh my blow tube between my notebook pages and try to look natural.

At that moment, the door opens. It's Brielle, back from delivering papers. She always takes her sweet time running errands. Why does she get away with stuff like that when I can't so much as flip a water bottle without getting called out?

Brielle makes eye contact with Ms. Campbell as she enters the room. Then she steps on a marshmallow.

Please play it cool, Brielle. Please.

"Ugh!" Her blond hair sweeps in front of her face as she examines the bottom of her lacy white sandals. "Why is there a marshmallow on the floor? Wait. Let me guess. Jack."

Whyyyyyyy, Brielle? Why?! It's a marshmallow, not dog poop. Does she really have to make a scene?

Ms. Campbell's gaze moves slowly from Brielle's shoe to me. I press my lips together, feeling my skin begin to melt under the heat of her laser eyes.

"Jack, were you shooting marshmallows at me?"

I can't just lie. That would make me a coward. Part of being the class clown is owning up to your practical jokes.

"Yeah," I admit. I try to look relaxed even though my heart's pounding so hard, my throat can feel it.

Ms. Campbell closes her eyes for a couple of seconds. "Why would you do that?"

I look left and right. "Um . . . I thought you might be hungry?" A couple of kids snort quietly, which eases the sting of embarrassment.

Sometimes Ms. Campbell will chuckle along with comments like that, but not today. She puts her hands on her hips and frowns. "See me after class. And for not speaking up, the rest of you will wait in silence for one minute after the bell. I am very disappointed right now."

Disappointed. The ultimate guilt trip. A few people shoot

17

me dirty looks, but almost everyone else stares at their desk in shame.

Brielle slips back into her seat and straightens her pencils in front of her notebook. Thanks to Miss Perfectionist, now everybody hates me. Being held captive in the room after the bell rings is miserable.

"And, Zane," Ms. Campbell says as she grabs a stack of books off her desk, "I'll see you after class too. I saw the phone; now put it away."

The tips of Zane's ears become strawberry red, and he turns to glare at me. He pulls the phone out from between his thighs and shoves it into his front pocket. The look on his face tells me this friendship is no longer just fizzling out. It's completely over.

3

Why So Serious?

During the minute of silence after class, I keep my eyes glued to my desk. If anyone else is glaring at me, I don't want to see.

"Your minute's over," Ms. Campbell says, and everyone shoots out the door like a stink bomb just exploded. I consider making a run for it myself. I don't usually mind being lectured, but today feels different.

Zane and I walk up to Ms. Campbell's desk. She sets her pencil down and looks me in the eye. "When I'm teaching, I don't like distractions, Jack. I feel I have been patient with you all year, but shooting marshmallows at me crosses a line."

My stomach feels squirmy, like a bucket of worms. I don't even get why. This isn't a huge deal. It's not like mini marshmallows could hurt anyone.

"I'm sorry, Ms. Campbell. I just thought it would be funny."

"Well, I wish you had considered how I'd feel."

My stomach twists again, and I look down. I like Ms. Campbell. I didn't mean to make her hate me.

"For your consequence," she continues, "I'll have to take ten points off your citizenship grade and write you up for lunch detention on Monday."

I shift my weight from one foot to the other. "Okay."

Ms. Campbell turns her attention to Zane. "I'm taking five points off your citizenship grade and giving you lunch detention as well."

Zane's mouth drops open. "But I didn't do anything!"

"I understand it feels like you weren't a part of this, but by recording, you made yourself an accomplice." She rubs her temples. "I know you boys enjoy making your videos, but you really should think twice before you hit Record, Zane. Even when your friend encourages you to."

Zane stiffens. "We're not friends." Wow, way to kick me in the gut.

Ms. Campbell glances at me, and worry wrinkles form around her eyes. She sighs and looks back at Zane. "I'm going to ask you to erase the video. Do you understand why I don't want that on the internet? It makes me feel very disrespected."

Zane grumbles an apology. He takes out his phone, and Ms. Campbell watches him delete the video.

"Thank you." She writes us each a tardy slip for our next classes. "I'll see you both on Monday."

All this negativity is cramping my style. Once Zane and I are in the hallway, I try to lighten the mood. I lean over and whisper, "You have the backup video, right?"

"Not funny," Zane says, looking straight ahead.

"I was just kidding."

"You're always just kidding. You're so immature."

"Imma-*ture*?" I say with a British accent. That's not anything I haven't heard before. "Well, I'd rather be imma-*ture* than totally unable to take a joke. What's your deal today?"

"Nothing." He's halfway yelling now. "I just didn't want to take that video, okay?"

"It's not like I forced you."

"Well, you asked in front of everybody. I'm sick of recording you all the time. I'm sick of *you*."

And there's the kick to the gut, part two. So he's sick of me. My suspicions have been confirmed. Instead of feeling mopey about it, I'm starting to get angry.

I block his path. "What about the talent show?"

"What about it?"

"You're just gonna ditch out?"

"Obviously. You don't even have a plan."

"I do too," I say.

The plan was to think of a plan.

I soften my voice and try to sound reasonable. "Come on. People are expecting us to do something. I teased it on my MyTube channel last night."

"News flash: no one cares about your MyTube channel. You're not even that funny."

Kick to the gut, part three. My gut can't take any more kicking, but I can't let him see how much that hurt, so I scoff. "My thousands of followers would beg to differ."

"Then ask one of them," he says, and walks away.

"Maybe I will."

"Whatever," he calls over his shoulder. "Good luck finding someone dumb enough to hang out with you."

"*You* were one of those dumb people!" I say, and then realize I just low-key insulted myself. "I mean . . . you were smart before, but dumb now. Because, like, it wasn't dumb to hang out with me, and . . . yeah!"

He's already turned the corner.

The bell rings, signaling the start of second period. I stand motionless in the hallway, surrounded by nothing but the usual smell of Lysol and lingering B.O. Suddenly I feel heavy. And kind of sick. I lean against the wall and slide down to sit.

Congratulations to me. I've managed to make an enemy

of one of the most popular guys at school. What if he decides to turn people against me? I lean my forehead on my knees. Zane's a jerk. I should have seen this coming. He never even wore the hedgehog socks I got him for his birthday. What kind of a person doesn't like hedgehogs?

He's right about one thing, though. I should just ask someone else to do the talent show. Someone cooler than him. We'll do something totally awesome that everyone will be talking about. Then Zane will regret what he said.

A lot of people around school watch my videos. I get along with almost everyone, but I don't know who'd be willing to actually get on a stage with me. The tryouts are next Thursday, and the show is a little over two weeks later. I'd need to find someone who wouldn't ditch out between now and then.

And *that*, apparently, is the hard part.

I shift, and something crinkles on my back. I reach behind me and pull out a paper flyer. I must have dragged it when I slid down the wall.

"Come to Speed Friendshipping!" the flyer says in bright green letters. "Sparkling conversations—New friends—Doughnuts galore." It's the meet-your-new-bestie event from the announcements.

Earlier, in class, I thought this sounded super cheesy. But now I'm intrigued. Maybe one of these speed friendshippers would do the show with me. I could scope out my options and pick someone who actually has a sense of humor. It might be my best shot.

But if I go to speed friendshipping, people might think I'm desperate.

Nah. I'll just pretend I'm there for the free doughnuts.

I send a text to my mom.

"I'm going to a club thing after school. I'll message when it's over."

Let the search begin.

4

The World's Most Effective Bait

After school, I head to the drama room. "Hey!" I shout down the crowded hallway. "Anyone going to speed friend-shipping?"

I point to Jenna Rancher, who's pulling her backpack from her locker, and speak like a talk-show host. "Would *you* like to find a soul friend?"

"Ha." She shakes her head. "I can't miss the bus."

"Would *you* like to find a soul friend?" I say to Jax Sanchez, who's huddled with a group of friends by the bulletin board.

He laughs. "Dude, come on, no one's going to that."

"*Whaaaat?*" I snap across the air. "It's gonna be the bomb!

I'm gonna meet my soul friend. And eat doughnuts!" I can't look like I'm taking this too seriously. If I show up quietly, it'll look like I honestly want to find a friend.

Which is true, but that's beside the point.

When I get to the drama room, I swing the door open and jump inside. "I heard there were doughnuts in here."

Mr. Busby, the school's guidance counselor, tilts his head and gives me a twinkly-eyed smile. Behind him, the words "You belong here" are written in cursive on the whiteboard. Mr. Busby wears dark jeans and a slim green suit coat—the type of thing you can only pull off if you're young and trendy like he is. I had to talk with him back in January after a certain slip-and-slide-down-the-hallway incident, probably to make sure I didn't have a deeply troubled mind. (For the record, I knew squirting bubble solution onto the linoleum and penguin-sliding down the hall wasn't the *best* idea, but I never expected it would classify as a criminal offense.)

Mr. Busby turned out to be pretty cool, though. We mostly talked about my family and movies and stuff like that. He said I could visit him anytime I wanted, but I haven't. If people found out I met with the counselor, I'm not sure what they'd think, and I'd rather not find out.

Next to Mr. Busby, Principal Duncan crosses his arms and frowns. I'm 89 percent sure he hates my guts. He used to say hi to me in the halls last year when I first started sixth grade, but that's probably because he thought I'd be like my older brother. Jacob got straight A's and was in charge of some service club before he went to high school.

"Take a seat." Principal Duncan motions to two rows of chairs lined up facing each other. One row has green chairs and the other has red. A jar of Popsicle sticks sits on the desk between each set of chairs.

As expected, there aren't many people. Maybe thirteen, tops. I recognize some of them from my classes, like this new girl Tasha, who I've never heard speak, and this kid with short red hair who I think farted in history once. A few other people went to my elementary school, but they had a different teacher.

Instead of taking a seat, I jump and swat at one of the silver star cutouts dangling from the ceiling. "Can I pick the song?"

Principal Duncan's nose twitches, and his frown line deepens. "What are you talking about?"

"We're playing musical chairs, right? I wanna pick the song." I turn to the people in the chairs. "I dominate this game. But I did break a kid's finger once by sitting on it, so watch out, guys."

A single chuckle breaks the silence. Tough crowd. No one here is the type who would appreciate my jokes. Maybe coming was a mistake.

Good thing getting out of things with ridiculous excuses is my forte. That, and pretending I really have to use the bathroom, which could be plan B.

I slide over to Mr. Busby and tap his shoulder. "Hey, Buzz. I just remembered I have this really important thing where I have to groom my gerbil. Can I grab my doughnut and leave?"

"Doughnuts are for those who stay the whole time. Your gerbil will have to wait."

I peek at the doughnuts. Are they worth it?

Through the box's plastic window, I see that they're powdered jelly doughnuts.

I must stay.

"Well played," I mumble to Mr. Busby. I take the green seat in front of the quiet girl, Tasha. As hopeless as it seems, I might as well try to find a talent show partner here. Time's running out, and I don't exactly have applicants lining up at my locker.

Principal Duncan welcomes the room and thanks us for coming. He says we're going to learn "interpersonal skills that, as we grow, will aid us in both our professional and personal lives." Way to turn this into something that sounds super boring, dude.

Next Mr. Busby talks about "nonverbal communication," which is basically the way you act and sound when you talk. He pulls up a volunteer—the redheaded possible farter, whose name, it turns out, is Perry. Mr. Busby sits across from him, and they role-play what "good" and "bad" nonverbal communication look like. The bad example is super funny. Mr. Busby keeps crossing his arms, checking his phone, and fake-picking his nose.

Mr. Busby sends Perry back to his seat and then stands in front of the whiteboard. "While you're chatting, remember this: Put your phone away. Look your partner in the eye. Smile. Nod. Show them that what they're saying is interesting. Because it will be! There's nothing more interesting than people." He writes that last sentence on the board and makes us repeat it like we're being brainwashed.

Mr. Busby holds up a silver bell with a dinger—the kind you see on store counters. "When I ring this, one partner will draw a Popsicle stick and ask the other partner the written question. Ask follow-up questions so you don't run out of things to say. You'll have two minutes. Try to switch turns about halfway through. When time's up, I'll ring the bell. The green row will shift down one seat, and we'll repeat the process. Ready?"

Right as he's about to ring the bell, the door opens and wouldja look who it is: Miss Perfect Brielle.

"I'm sorry I'm late," she says between gasps of air, her white skin turning slightly pink. She gives the principal puppy-dog eyes. "I had to talk to a teacher after school. I rushed to get here. I—"

Principal Duncan waves his hand at her and beams. "Don't worry about it. We are *so* happy to have you here. I'll be your partner and fill you in on what we're doing."

"Oh, thank you!" Brielle says. "I knew you were my favorite principal for a reason." What a teacher's pet.

She sits at the end of the row and smooths the wrinkles in her flowy, light pink skirt. Honestly, I'm surprised she came. It's not like she's lacking in the friend department. She probably wants to put this on a résumé or something.

"One more thing," Principal Duncan says as he takes the seat across from Brielle. "The goal here is to have fun, but also to create school unity. As an extra challenge, try setting up a time to get together with one person. Just one."

Mr. Busby bobs his head in agreement. "Great suggestion."

Like that's gonna happen. These two seem to think it's so easy to set up friend dates with people you don't even know.

Mr. Busby dings the bell. "Begin."

My partner, Tasha, tugs on her crocheted hat. Today it's purple, to match her long-sleeved shirt. Tasha has, like, a bajillion hats, always in different shades and styles. I swear she's worn a new one every day since she moved here. If you look at the spot right above her neck, you'll see that her hair is shaved real close to the scalp. I wonder if she's sick, like in this one movie I saw where the girl had cancer and lost all her hair. It would probably be rude to ask.

I crack my knuckles. "Let's get friendshipping. I friend-ship so hard."

Tasha smirks and opens her mouth like she's about to joke back, but then decides against it. "So . . . Do you want to go first or me?"

This is the first time I've heard her voice. It's not as soft as I expected. "Either way."

She reaches for a stick, and purple mini pom-poms dangle from the ends of her sleeves. I have a strange urge to bat at them like a cat.

Tasha looks over the Popsicle stick and then fixes her wide brown eyes on me. She reads in an interested tone, "What are some of your favorite hobbies?"

I lean back in my chair. "Easy. Grooming my imaginary gerbil. Sleeping. Eating marshmallows. Next question."

"We're only supposed to ask one question per round."

"Hey, Buzz," I shout to Mr. Busby, who's checking the timer on his phone. "What prize do we win if we answer the most questions in one round?"

"Only one Popsicle stick per round. And the prize is getting to know your partner better."

Mr. Busby's chill enough to mess with, so I hop out of my seat. "There's no prize money?! I demand a refund!"

Principal Duncan speaks firmly from the end of the row. "Jack, one more outburst and I'm going to ask you to leave."

I failed to consider all the adults in the room. Principal Duncan is the *opposite* of chill.

Mr. Busby points at me with a fake-angry face. "Play nicely or no doughnut."

I sit back down and grumble. I hate that the powdery goodness has so much control over me, but I can't resist its power.

Tasha raises her eyebrow like she thinks I'm some weirdo. Then she clears her throat and folds her arms over the desk. "Well, as for my hobbies, I like to read. Mostly fantasy. And I like fashion design."

I nod. "Cool."

She nods too. "Yeah."

We sit in silence for a bit, avoiding eye contact. I'm pretty sure we look exactly like Mr. Busby's example of bad nonverbal communication, but I don't have anything else to say. The kids next to us are done with their conversation too, and the chatter in the room dwindles down to a few mumbly voices.

Wasn't this only supposed to be two minutes? It feels like much longer. I slip my phone halfway out of my pocket to check the time. The teachers don't call me out for it, so I quickly check MyTube to see if anyone's posted about my marshmallow darts. Jax Sanchez's story shows him shooting a marshmallow down the hall. The trend didn't catch on at the beginning of the year, but maybe now that there's only a month left, it will.

Ding! The bell finally rings. "Rotate," shouts Mr. Busby.

I say bye to Tasha and move down the aisle. The guy across from me is the only dude that laughed at my musical-chairs joke earlier. His wavy hair covers his light brown forehead, and he wears a plain blue T-shirt. I don't remember ever seeing him around, but he looks a little familiar.

"'Sup?" I say.

"Hey. I'm Mario."

"As in *Mario Kart*?"

"Never heard *that* one before."

"You're right. I can do better." I squint and think real hard. "How about: Is your brother named Luigi?"

"Heard it."

"Is your girlfriend's name Peach?"

"Weak."

"Do you have a pet *Toad*?"

He snorts. "Okay, that was decent. But I'm not named after a video game. I'm named after my dad. And my grandpa. And, like, three other old dudes in my family."

"That's cool, I guess. I'm named after Jack in the Box. My mom went into labor eating a cheeseburger."

He laughs pretty loud. I'm thinking he's a good candidate for my talent show partner-slash-possible-new-friend.

Mario reaches for a Popsicle stick and I say, "Hey," before his hand reaches the jar. This is feeling too normal to ruin it with one of those awkward conversation starters.

I lean in and speak quietly, like people in movies do when they're proposing a secret mission. "Would you or would you not be interested in achieving internet fame and fortune?"

He squints. "Huh?"

"You know, like, going viral. Making a video that gets lots of shares."

He scratches his eyebrow. "I . . . guess?"

This is looking semi-promising. At least he's not saying no.

"One minute left," Mr. Busby shouts. I've got to explain in turbo speed.

"Here's the deal. I've been teasing that I'd do this super-cool stunt for the talent show and post it on my MyTube. But my partner bailed last minute, so I'm looking for someone to take his place."

"What's the stunt?"

"About that . . . I'm not sure. But I have some ideas. And we could brainstorm."

"I'm pretty good at hacky sack."

"That would be perfect for the tryouts!"

His eyebrows shoot up. "Oh yeah?"

"Wanna do some planning tomorrow?" I pull my phone out. "I can give you my number." I can't believe I'm actually setting up a "friend date," like Principal Duncan suggested. It's less awkward than I expected.

"Sure." Mario looks genuinely happy. This could be my guy! I can't believe I found him so quickly. Maybe finding that speed-friendshipping poster was fate.

Ding! goes the bell.

"We're not done yet!" I shout, and then I remember Principal Duncan's no-outbursts rule. I hunch my shoulders and mouth, "Sorry," in his direction. He cringes in return.

Mr. Busby chuckles. "You can talk more when this is over. Rotate!"

I glance at my next partner and grumble deep in my throat.

Next up is two minutes with Brielle, and I'm thinking, no thanks.

5

Compliment Fail

I know it's not technically Brielle's fault that I got in trouble earlier. Ms. Campbell would've noticed the marsh-mallows eventually, and since they're my signature snack, they would've outed me as the culprit.

But still, Brielle threw me under the bus like she didn't even care. She could've at least said sorry when she realized she got me in trouble.

I take my seat and force a tight-lipped smile. I can't make a big deal out of this. It's whatever. Besides, you don't want a girl like Brielle to go around talking bad about you. People would take her side just because she's cute and popular.

Brielle flashes a smile, showing off teeth worthy of a toothpaste commercial. "Hey, Jack."

"Hey," I say, and then turn to Mario. "Dude, put your number in my phone."

Mr. Busby pops up behind us like a ninja. He blocks my phone with his hand before I can pass it to Mario. "No phones during speed friendshipping. Focus on your partner."

Brielle frowns and clacks her nails on the desk. The tips are painted white and the rest peachy pink—that one style that makes your nails look like regular nails, but upgraded.

"Well," Brielle says. "Go ahead and draw a Popsicle stick. I drew first last turn." I feel like she's my mom giving me orders, but I do it anyway.

The question on the Popsicle stick is super awkward. I'd invent another question, but Mr. Busby is staring over my shoulder like a creeper, so he'd know.

I try not to grimace. "Give your new friend three sincere compliments."

Brielle takes a deep breath. You can tell she's not too thrilled about this either. She smiles sweetly—probably to please Mr. Busby. "Okay. For one, you always have interesting socks."

I slap my ankle onto the desk and tug up the bottom of my jeans. "Yesterday I had turtle socks, which were way cooler. They're just checkered today."

"Exactly. Like I said, interesting."

Deep down, I bet she's thinking she wouldn't be caught dead wearing these socks. It must be killing her to find ways

to compliment me. I lean forward and grin. "Keep 'em coming. I love being flattered."

She blinks. "You can be pretty funny." Not original, but it's still nice to hear after Zane's diss this morning.

Mr. Busby walks off to listen in on other conversations. Brielle pauses, and for a moment I think she won't finish now that the teacher's not watching. Finally, she says, "It seems like you're really confident."

Confident? Is that code for conceited?

"Why do you say that?"

She does a Brielle version of a shrug, where she lifts one shoulder and tilts her head toward it. "I don't know. You're not afraid to be yourself. You never seem embarrassed by anything."

I was embarrassed today, I want to say, *when you totally called me out in front of the class.*

"Thanks," I mumble. "Um . . . guess it's my turn."

I don't know Brielle well, so I don't know what kind of compliments she wants. I refuse to say she's nice. I can't say she's pretty or she might think I like her. This is harder than I thought.

"You have nice hair," is what I come up with. "It's, like, always . . . not messy, I guess."

She smiles and combs through her hair with her fingers. "Thanks."

"Number two." I glance at the clock on the wall, wishing Mr. Busby would ding the bell. "You have nice clothes."

Her smile droops, but I don't get why.

"And three . . ." I want to make this one good, since it was sort of nice she called me confident.

"Don't think about it too hard," Brielle mumbles, her smile completely gone.

"I got it. You never get in trouble."

She scoffs. "I've gotten in trouble before."

"Oh yeah?" I wiggle my eyebrows. "Let me guess. You were chewing gum."

"No."

"Sharpened your pencil without asking?"

"If you must know, my friend was talking to me during the lesson in science."

"And the teacher shushed you? *Oooooh*, hard core."

"Yeah, yeah, you're hilarious." She rolls her eyes.

"Hey." I lift my palms. "I'm not insulting you. I wish *I* got in less trouble."

Brielle bites her lip. "Serious question, though." She looks at the corner of the desk before she meets my eye. "Do you think it's . . . *boring* for someone to never get in trouble?"

Brielle's eyes are wide and pleading, like she expects me to give some deep response to her, honestly, kind of weird question. "I don't know," I say.

She twiddles her thumbs. "Like, I heard you ask Mario if he would do some crazy thing for the talent show. How did you know he'd be okay with doing that? Why would you ask him instead of, like . . . me, for example?"

"I don't know. Because I wouldn't think you'd want to. Why? Do you?"

"Well, no. But that's not the point."

I don't get it. But I don't want to dig into it either. This conversation is starting to feel weird. Where is that bell? Did Mr. Busby forget about it?

Ding!

Perfect timing.

I shoot out of my seat and knock on Brielle's desk before shifting down. "Nice chat." I shake my finger at her. "Now, watch that talking in class, young lady."

She looks at the ceiling and shakes her head.

Compared to the Brielle conversation, the next rounds of speed friendshipping go by smoothly and quickly. I learn

40

that Larissa has a pet weasel, Michael plays the violin, and Mei-ling wants to go to Sweden. I reach for my phone a couple of times, but then I remember phones are against the rules and stop myself.

Can you believe it? Me. Following the rules. My mother would be so proud.

For the last round, we have to pair up with someone in our same row, which is too bad because I'd rather talk to Mario again. I dash over to Perry before everyone else is taken so I don't get stuck with the principal. Perry and I talk about video games, and he lists, like, ten different zombie games off the top of his head. Even if he did fart in history, he turns out to be all right.

"Time's up!" Mr. Busby says while Perry's going on about gaming equipment. "You guys did so well!"

"Did anyone make plans to meet up outside of school?" Principal Duncan asks.

I raise my hand. "Mario and I are chillin' tomorrow. Chillin' like villains."

You'd think he'd be more proud of us, but Principal Duncan doesn't smile. "That's great, boys. Anyone else?"

His eyes pan the room in silence.

"Lookee here." I fold my arms. "Mario and I are the only ones who completed the extra challenge. Guess that makes us star students, huh? Air-five!" Mario air-fives me from a few desks over.

Principal Duncan rubs his chin. "Brielle, what about you?"

Brielle's eyes dart left and right a couple of times. "Um." She smiles at Tasha, who is sitting across from her. "Tasha and I had a good conversation. I'd love to hang out sometime." She tugs on a strand of hair. "Want me to let you know next time my friends get together?"

Tasha bounces her knee. "Um. Yeah, cool."

That was awkward for everybody.

Mr. Busby claps once. "What can I say? You guys are superstars. I really hope you all come back next week. We'll throw in some surprises, do things a little differently each time. We'd love a bigger turnout, so spread the word."

I lift a finger. "Might I suggest bringing pizza?"

He pulls his wallet from his suit coat, opens it, and winces. "Unfortunately, I don't believe I have the funds for that."

"Look, man, you gotta make cuts somewhere. This is important."

He snaps the wallet shut. "I'll think about what treats to bring next time. In the meantime, enjoy the doughnuts." Everyone rushes to the boxes, except for Brielle, who's in a conversation with the principal, naturally.

I grab the biggest doughnut and take a bite. Thick coconut custard overpowers my taste buds. Not the worst, but not the best.

"Huh," I say with my mouth full. "I thought these were gonna be jelly."

Mr. Busby crinkles his eyes. "Each doughnut has a unique surprise inside. Just like people."

I swallow another bite. "Kind of weird to compare people to something edible, but whatever."

After I finish the doughnut, Mario and I exchange numbers.

"It's technically my mom's number," Mario says, scratching the back of his neck. "But she'll let me know what you say."

Gotta remember to not send Mario any weird GIFs.

On my walk home, I pull up MyTube and post a talent show countdown to the top corner of my personal page. Twenty-two days left. That's plenty of time to come up with something awesome. I'll have to think of ideas to run by Mario tomorrow. We're bound to come up with something better than Zane and I would have. That'll show him.

Tasha

Tasha:

I thought someone might finally ask about my shaved head at speed friendshipping today. I mean, it seems like the first thing you'd notice about me. But no one did. I guess since we were focusing on the Popsicle-stick questions, it never came up. Or maybe everyone's scared that I have some terminal disease, and they don't want to remind me about it. As if I'd be able to forget if I did.

To be honest, sometimes I think my hair's the reason it's been so hard for me to find friends since I moved here. But I'm not ready to grow it out. Not yet.

It's been nearly six months since my big brother, DeAndre, died, and somehow, keeping my head shaved helps me feel connected to him. It's a constant reminder that life is short.

Before he got sick, DeAndre always prided himself on his hair. And for good reason. He had this super-cool high-top fade, with squiggly designs shaved into the sides. He'd comb through the top with his fingers and pick out the curls with an Afro pick. It was an art

44

form. When his hair started falling out from the chemo, it was like a part of his personality fell away too.

I shaved my head the same day he did. Anything to feel just a fragment of what he was going though. I still remember the empty hum of the buzzer as chunks of my black hair floated to the floor. Later that week, Grandma sat me down at her kitchen table. "I taught you how to sew," she said. "Now you're going to learn to crochet." With her help, I made matching hats for DeAndre and me. That made him smile again. I'd get armfuls of yarn from the dollar store and make funky patterns with surprising colors. DeAndre especially loved playing with the little pom-poms I sewed to the edges of our hats. "You're destined to be a fashion designer," he said. I've been working on it ever since.

It'd be nice to find someone I could talk with about this stuff, but moving to a new school near the end of the year feels like crashing a party that will be over in ten minutes anyway. The girls I sit with at lunch have been friends for years, so they're always laughing about jokes I wasn't there for or movies I haven't seen. I thought I'd have more of a connection with Kayla, since she's one of the only other black girls at this school, but so far, not really. Now Brielle says she'll text me to hang out, but she obviously just felt obligated in front of the principal.

Then there's Mom, who's only interested in discussing the home renovation. We're on our second live-in house flip, and hopefully our last. Those home flippers on TV always look like they're having fun, but in reality, it's sweaty, smelly, and so dusty it feels like drowning in quicksand. Needless to say, chatting after school sounded like a decent alternative to helping Mom patch drywall.

Things started out a little weird talking to Jack. He obviously just came to mess around. Jack's the kind of guy that elicits eye rolls, but you can't help but like him anyway. He's got wild curly hair, constant energy, and a permanent smirk on his freckly face. He comes up with all these goofy ideas, and people follow him just because he's him. Once, he got everyone in our math class to start sniffing every time the teacher faced the whiteboard. Ms. Snyder got so fed up that she passed around a box of Kleenex and forced everyone to blow their noses. He makes class interesting; that's for sure. It's too bad he can't hold much of a conversation past making jokes.

The other rounds were better, though. It was nice to have conversations that didn't include a single mention of drywall or spackling techniques.

And that boy Mario was pretty cute. I wonder if he'll be back next week.

Mario:

"Perry Skousen? That guy's such a weirdo."

That's what Zane Peterson said in math yesterday. He was talking to the guy beside him, but I over-heard since they both sit behind me. I should have turned around and defended Perry. After all, he's my best friend.

Or, at least, I'm his.

But the terrible part—and I hate admitting this—is that Perry *is* kind of a weird dude. Of course, it's not something you should go around saying (and I do re-gret not telling Zane to shove it), but I can't help but wonder: if people think Perry's a weirdo, and I hang around him all the time, do I become a weirdo too?

If Perry were a better friend, I might be okay with that. But this past year, things have felt different. Our parents are friends, so we grew up together doing all that kid stuff like selling lemonade and playing with the hose on the trampoline. But lately, he's gotten way into video games and that's *allll* he ever wants to do. I'd rather play soccer or hacky sack or *do* stuff. He only wants to sit around and game or watch others game online.

I probably sound like such a jerk. In books and

Mario

47

movies, it's always the jerk who wants to ditch their friend.

Ditch sounds so harsh. I just want to move on.

I want to be nice about it, so I suggested we go to speed friendshipping. Best-case scenario is he meets someone he has more in common with, and so do I. We could stay kind-of friends, but not hang out anymore.

Is that so bad? Are we required to be besties for the rest of our lives just because we grew up on the same street?

Jack wants to hang out tomorrow, and to be honest, I'm pretty stoked. I know he hangs around Zane, but Jack seems a lot nicer. He started the T-rexing thing, and seems to be a pretty cool dude.

Hopefully he's not weirded out that I don't have a phone. That was embarrassing to admit when he asked for my number. Everyone's always talking about their group chats and their MyTube accounts, and I'm always left out because I have the strictest mom in the world.

I wonder if Jack will like hacky sack.

Brielle:

The knot in my stomach that was supposed to loosen after speed friendshipping is still there. As I walk through the school doors, I pull out my phone and add one more item to my to-do list.

Brielle

WEEKEND TO-DOS:

Make cuter student council posters

Post makeup tutorial to MyTube

Church leadership meeting Sunday at 9

Finish homework—prioritize social studies essay!

Get page protectors

Make cookies for young women who missed church

Send Honor Club budget report to principal

Do something with Tasha

It didn't even seem like Tasha wanted to hang out. But I said I'd text her, and if there's one thing I pride myself on, it's that I follow through. Always.

Plus, if word got out that "snotty Brielle ditched out on some poor, less popular soul," then The Situation could get worse.

49

The knot in my stomach tightens. It doesn't help that all I've had time to eat today is a granola bar and a cheese stick. I would've taken that doughnut, but Mom and I are trying to reduce our sugar intake.

Mom texts me that she's on her way, so I sit on the curb and pull up MyTube to check for new comments. My heart races when I see the pile of new notifications. Luckily, all of them are likes or tags. No trolls.

In my most recent post, I'm showing off the new lipstick Mom got me. It's the kind of shade that looks great in photos but would be way too intense for school—a dark, pigmented burgundy. I got lots of likes, but not as many as my best friend, Devyn. Her last photo is her with her long hair and perfect, dark brown skin lying on some beach in the middle of the Caribbean. Devyn's family is always vacationing—they even went on this cruise right in the middle of the school year—so naturally, her photos get more attention. She might be prettier than me too. She definitely has a cuter swimsuit.

I add one more thing to my to-do list: ask Mom for a new swimsuit.

Still, the lipstick selfie's a good pic. The photo editor was able to hide my zit and make my eyelashes longer. But maybe it's *too* good, if you know what I mean. Like I'm trying too hard. I've been going back and forth on whether to delete it since first period.

During English, Ms. Campbell sent me to deliver some papers, and on my way back, I stopped in the bathroom to check my phone. Phones are kinda-sorta banned in the hallways, but I've never heard a teacher explicitly say not to use them in the bathroom.

At least not to my face. (It's, like, the one rule I break, okay?)

I leaned against the sink, caught up on a couple of group chats, and pulled up MyTube. That's when I saw a comment from an anonymous account.

It said, "Brielle is soooo pretty. Pretty BORING."

My heart sagged a couple of inches and just kind of hung there.

It got worse.

Someone had replied to them. A private account that only posts GIFs and memes.

They said, "Girl thinks she's all that and a bag of chips."

My throat squeezed a little, and I felt the cry coming on. I knew I couldn't show up to English with mascara streaks, so I gulped hard and dabbed at my eyes with tissue. Seven people had liked the "boring" comment, and two others liked the "bag of chips" comment.

Nine people agree that I'm boring and think I'm all that.

I didn't recognize their names. They could be randos from other schools, or they could be people I know who have fake accounts. I don't even know who to trust. I deleted the comments, not wanting to see how many likes they could rack up.

When I told Devyn about it at lunch, she rolled her eyes. "It's, like, two bad comments among a bajillion compliments. For real, Bri."

She was right. But sometimes I suspect that the people complimenting me don't mean it.

The trolls definitely meant it.

Devyn put her hand on mine. "You're going to get haters if you want a big following. Why not just make your account private?"

It sounded like a good idea. With a private account, I wouldn't always have to block creepers and spammy bots, and I wouldn't have to worry about people stealing and reposting my content.

But my account wouldn't grow. I'm aiming for three thousand followers by the end of the school year. Thanks to my makeup tutorials, I have more followers than anyone at school. Except for Jack, surprisingly. He's always throwing marshmallows and acting like strange animals and eating gross foods. His videos are immature, but he's amusing enough.

"We could both make our accounts private," I suggested to Devyn.

She sipped her vitamin water. "I don't care if I get haters—*you* do. I'm not going private."

If she's not, then neither am I.

All day, I haven't been able to look at people the same. Whenever I pass someone in the halls, I wonder if it could have been them. What if there are tons of people who secretly hate me?

If that's true, there's no way I'll win as student body president.

That's why I came to speed friendshipping. I wanted to branch out to new people; let them know I'm not stuck up. It was exhausting. I had to smile and nod and look interested in everything everyone said. It's not that I dislike people. I just hate making small talk with people I don't know. Zane Peterson's my rival for president, and he doesn't talk to people outside of his group either, but I've never heard anyone say anything bad about him. It's seriously not fair.

So, now I have to hang out with Tasha. It's not that I don't like her. She seems nice, kind of like a spunky fashionista with the shaved head/bright hat thing she's got going on. But, like, seriously? I already have soooo much to do. How can I possibly squeeze her in?

Mom's blue Suburban pulls up. I stand quickly and get so dizzy that I almost fall back onto the curb. When I hop into the car, my stomach roars like a dragon.

I really should've taken a doughnut.

6

In a Jam

On Saturday, I wake to the sweet smell of waffles—a sign it's gonna be a good day. I rush to the kitchen without changing out of my pajamas or brushing my teeth. In a house of three boys, you've gotta fight your way to the food.

In the kitchen, Jacob and Josh are already eating at the table. (Yes, we are Jacob, Jack, and Josh—one of *those* families that name all their kids with the same first letter. It confuses teachers for the first week of school, but they learn my name quickly. I make them say it enough.)

The waffle plate on the counter is left with only crumbs. *Fish sticks*. Dad's pouring another batch into the waffle maker, so it'll be a couple of minutes. "Morning, Jack," he says, wiping his hands on the dorky green apron Mom got him for Christmas. Dad's a sous-chef for the Hilton hotel in town, which means he's second-in-command to the head chef. I think he's good enough to be the head himself. His waffles are the perfect combination of fluffy and crispy.

"Come get some eggs," Dad says. Eggs aren't my favorite, but I'm starving. I dish some out of the frying pan with a spatula and sit next to Jacob. His plate is easy to steal from because he's too much of a health freak to make a scene if I sneak a forkful of waffle.

Jacob buries his nose in his biology textbook while his half-eaten plate sits out in the open, calling my name. I down the rest of his waffle in three gigantic bites. It's dry because there's no syrup on it. What kind of monster eats waffles without syrup?

Jacob's a track star at the high school and a perfect student. He's probably the only guy in the world who'd rather be studying on a Saturday morning than finishing his waffles. I heard there's some study showing that the oldest child is usually the smartest, and in the case of my family, that's true.

Jacob's smart in a schoolish sense, anyway. Not in the important ways. He never understands the memes I show him, and I have to explain why they're funny, which totally kills the joke. I don't get the point of the "smartest child" study anyway. Was it really so important for those "scientists" to tell the world that firstborns usually have a few more IQ points? It's like they wanted to make everyone else feel bad. I bet a firstborn created that study.

"Hey, Jack," says my younger brother, Josh. "Look what I got Dad to buy me with my lawn-mowing money." He props his leg on my chair and pulls his pant leg up.

I squint at the pattern on his socks. "Are those . . ."

"Cheez-Its!" he yells. "Sweet, huh?"

Now I see it. It's like someone printed the cover of a Cheez-Its box on a pair of socks. I hate that I didn't find those first. I try to not look impressed, even though I obviously am.

"I can't believe those exist," I say.

"Dude, we have the internet," he says. "*Everything* exists."

Josh is eleven, two years younger than me. When we were kids, he'd always follow me around, stealing my toys and my Superman costume, and copying everything I did. Unfortunately, he never grew out of it. After T-rexing made it big, Josh found a dinosaur costume at the thrift store and ran through the hallways of his elementary school *grawr-ing*. I secretly suspect that's why T-rexing has gotten less popular. Things aren't cool once the younger kids start doing them. Mom says, "Imitation is the best form of flattery," but I sometimes wish my style could just be *my* style, if you know what I mean. If Josh starts a funky sock trend in his fifth-grade class, then I might have to give mine up for good.

"Next batch is done!" Dad calls out as he stacks four

waffles on a plate. Josh and I race to the counter and stab at them with our forks. "I should get three!" I say. "You've already eaten!"

"No, two for me and two for you! It's only fair!"

I throw the fork on the counter and grab at his plate, but he dodges to the left.

Dad raises his voice. "If you boys don't cut it out, neither of you gets one. Take two each."

I shoot Josh a silent death glare as I sit at the table with my measly two waffles. Dad always takes Josh's side.

I drown my waffles in syrup and stab them with my fork, holding my phone in the other hand. Mario's coming over in an hour to brainstorm, and I need more ideas. Luckily, I know just who to turn to for inspiration.

Paxton Poker is the funniest dude on the planet. He's got millions of MyTube followers and posts videos of him doing random stupid stuff, usually in public. Like, one time he was digging through the trash cans at a park and pulling out expensive stuff that he'd planted in them. He'd make a big scene jumping around and talking about how the trash cans were gold mines. When he left, all these bystanders started digging through the trash cans, but they couldn't find anything. It was hilarious.

Lately he's been getting so big that he can't do public pranks, because people recognize him. Wouldn't that be sweet? Random strangers knowing who you are? Some people want to be a dentist or a lawyer when they grow up. I want to be Paxton Poker.

I scroll through his past videos. Which one of these could I change up and use as a talent somehow?

There's the classic video of him running through a sandwich shop in a gorilla suit. That one inspired T-rexing. I wish I had a gorilla suit, but they are ridiculously expensive, and I doubt I can find one at the thrift store. Josh got lucky with the dino costume.

Maybe Mario and I can dress up like something cheaper. We could be chickens. All we'd have to do is roll around in something sticky—syrup, maybe?—and then break a feather pillow over our heads. Even if we made ourselves into chickens, though, what would our talent be? Squawking?

Possibly. But I need more options.

In another video, Paxton and his friend sword-fight with French bread while simultaneously eating it. Maybe Mario and I can tape string cheese to our foreheads and try to see who can get the first bite off the other's string cheese. That would be fun.

Mom walks into the kitchen and rubs her eyes. She had a late shift working at the hospital last night, so her hair is frizzy and she's still in pj's. "Jack." She yawns. "Do you really have to use your phone at the table?"

"I'm doing research. For school."

Dad gives Mom a disgusting kiss on the lips and then

points at me. "Listen to your mother. I see that phone again, and I'm taking it for the rest of the day."

He means it, too. He's done it before. I slip my phone into my pocket and groan.

Josh puts his hand over his heart. "If *I* had a phone, I wouldn't use it at the table."

"No phone until you're twelve," Mom says as she takes a plate out of the cabinet. "You know the rule."

Josh grumbles. "Everyone at school has one."

"Everyone?" Mom says with fake surprise. "Well, then"— she sits next to him and ruffles his hair—"I guess I'm the meanest mom in the world. I can handle that."

Honestly, I wouldn't mind if Mom broke her no-phone-until-you're-twelve rule for Josh. His friends are always texting me when they want to hang out with him, and it's super annoying. He's always getting invited to stuff.

I don't know if I'm more jealous of that or his Cheez-It socks.

Over at the sink, Dad rinses the waffle-batter bowl and wipes his hands on his apron. Then he pulls out his phone and starts scrolling through it.

"Seriously?" I say. "You made me put *my* phone away."

Mom points at him with her fork. "He's got a point, hon."

"Sorry." Dad puts the phone back in his pocket. "I was searching for ways to keep raccoons away. Those darn pests keep digging through our trash."

"*I* know!" Josh says. "We get a girl raccoon doll and put it on the other end of the yard as a decoy."

Dad raises an eyebrow. "A girl raccoon doll? Does that even exist?"

"*Everything* exists," Josh and I say at the same time.

"What ideas have you found?" Mom asks Dad.

He butters up his waffle. "One site said to wrap a string of blinking Christmas lights around your bins. It's supposed to scare them off."

I snort. "Can we put giant Santa hats on them too?"

"Veto," Mom says. "I'll ask around at work if anyone's had to deal with raccoons."

Jacob hasn't glanced up from reading to chime in at all. I don't get why Mom doesn't make him put away his textbook. It's every bit as distracting as my phone was.

Dad takes the seat next to Mom and grabs the syrup. "Anyone want to go to the pond today? Weather's warm."

A family friend owns this algae-filled pond in the middle of nowhere about forty-five minutes away. Dad used to take us fishing there when we were younger, but now Jacob always has homework and Josh always has plans, so I'm the one who gets stuck going. It's fun for the first ten minutes, but there's no Wi-Fi, and we hardly ever catch fish, so it gets boring real quick.

"I've got homework and a project to work on," Jacob says, per usual.

"I'm going to Jeremiah's to play soccer," Josh says, also per usual.

"I've got plans with a friend too," I say. It feels good to have a real excuse.

"Which friend?" Mom asks. "Zane?"

The mention of Zane makes me want to upchuck my waffles. "No. His name's Mario."

Josh grins. "Like *Mario Kart*?" Of course he would think of the same joke I did. Now I can see how it wasn't that funny.

"If your friend wants to go to the lake, we can all go fishing," Dad suggests.

"We've gotta work on our talent show act. Maybe next week."

Mom narrows her eyes. "The talent show? You'd better not be planning something inappropriate."

"It will be appropriate." Although it depends on her definition of *appropriate*.

Mom sighs. "Whatever you decide, you have to run it by me first."

So this will have to be funny, but appropriate enough for Mom to approve. That sounds tough. I wonder if she'd be okay with the feathery squawking idea.

I finish my waffle, but I'm still hungry. It was totally unfair that Dad only let me take two. My eggs are cold, so I squeeze ketchup on them to spice them up. I take a bite, and—

"Blech!" I spit them out. "What the—?"

Jacob and Josh bust up laughing. I stare at my fork and it takes a few seconds to register: someone filled the ketchup bottle with raspberry jam.

"Come on," I say. "Who did this?"

"It was me, it was me," Josh says proudly, his hands in the air.

Mom looks like she's trying not to laugh. Dad looks less amused. "Josh, you'd better not have wasted the ketchup."

"The bottle was empty, I swear! I set it up, like, two days

ago. I can't believe it took so long for someone to use the ketchup."

"Pathetic," I say.

"More like genius," he says.

"It didn't even taste bad. I was just surprised."

"Yeah, right," Jacob says, finally closing his textbook. "You were totally grossed out."

Just to show them, I shove a big mouthful of raspberry eggs in my mouth and swallow. I've eaten my fair share of food combinations in my life. This is amateur stuff.

"You're gonna have to try harder if you want to gross me out." I pound my fork on the table and raise it in the air. "I'm the king of gross food combos."

An idea sparks in my mind, and I smile my most wicked grin.

I put my fork down. "I know exactly what I'm doing for the talent show."

7

The Dartboard of Doom

When Mario shows up, I lead him to my bedroom quickly before Josh tries to play some prank on him or Dad stops him to talk up the pond. "Whoa, your room is huge," he says at the doorway. He walks over to the couch and runs his hand across the blue cushions. "It's so cool you can fit this in here."

"Thanks. My dad found it at a yard sale, but we cleaned it real good."

One great thing about my parents is that they let us decorate our rooms however we want, within reason. I got turned down for a minifridge because it was "unnecessary," but I settled for a couch, a hanging dartboard, movie posters, and a neon lava lamp that's fun to stare at when I don't feel like doing anything.

Mario pulls two hacky sacks from the pocket of his gray sweatshirt. "I brought these so we could practice. I was thinking I could teach you a few tricks."

I guess it'd be good to get this part over with before I shock him with the awesome talent show idea I put together after breakfast.

He tosses me a yellow-and-green-striped hacky sack, and I catch it. "You kinda just kick these around, right?" I drop it onto my foot and kick it into the wall. It smacks so hard, I have to check that it didn't make a dent. Mom would kill me.

Mario laughs. "Not like that." He walks to the center of the room, drops his hacky sack, and starts kicking it like a pro. It bounces off the side of his foot, and he twists to catch it with his other foot. He lets it stall a half second before kicking it up again. The sack bounces around him like it has a life of its own, while Mario's legs crisscross to catch it.

"You're amazing!"

He finishes by taking off his baseball hat and using it to catch the sack. "And *that* is how you hacky-sack."

I give him a hearty round of applause. That was way cooler than I expected. "Teach me your ways, Jedi."

First Mario shows me how to kick the bag softly enough

that it doesn't bang into the wall. Then I move on to kicking it into my hand. I go for some more complicated moves, but no matter how hard I try, I can't kick the sack more than two times in a row. It just keeps plopping to the floor.

After fifteen minutes or so, I collapse into the couch. "I give up. I stink."

He stalls the sack on his knee and grabs it. "It's normal to not get it at first, but if you practice, like, ten, fifteen minutes every day, your feet will remember what to do. Muscle memory and all that."

Practice. I've never been much of a practicer. I'm so bad at practicing that my old piano teacher told my mom I should "find another hobby." Thank goodness, too, because she always smelled like cheese.

Cheese smells delightful under most circumstances. But not when mixed with old lady.

Practicing hacky sack every day sounds like a lot of work. I have a better idea.

I roll the hacky sack around on the arm of the couch. "My older brother, Jacob, played guitar for the talent show a couple of years ago. He says that they basically let everyone in. We don't have to be amazing, just decent enough to get through tryouts. You can do the hacky sack tricks, and I'll just, like, throw them to you."

"Yeah, no pressure. And then you'll have a couple of

weeks before the real show to get good enough to do your own tricks."

Uh-oh. He doesn't get it. Doesn't he remember my initial proposal to "achieve internet fame and fortune"? Hacky sack wouldn't do that for us.

I want to break it to him lightly, but I'm not sure how. "The hacky sack idea is just to get us through the tryouts, dude. We gotta pull something more original if we wanna go viral. That's the point, remember?"

"Right." His face starts to look a little droopy, like a melted ice cream cone.

"I mean, hacky sack is way cool, and you're super good, but I don't think it'll have the shock value that people are expecting. I mean, not unless we light them on fire or something."

"We technically could. There's this special hacky sack called the fire footbag that you can douse with kerosene and light up."

"That sounds awesome, but there's no way we'd get through tryouts playing with fire."

He frowns. "Yeah. My mom wouldn't let me either."

I reach for my dartboard, which is lying facedown on my bed. "Here's what I was thinking for the *real* show. I think this might be our ticket. Behold, the dartboard of doom!"

I hold up it up high and try not to look too dorkily proud of my creation. I've taped notebook paper all across the front of the board and labeled ten sections using different colored markers:

Pickles, eggs, garlic, dog food, tuna, Spam, Jell-O, spinach, cauliflower, syrup.

Mario sits on the edge of the couch. "Okay. I'm intrigued."

I put the board down. "Well, I realized today that one of the things I'm best at is eating gross food. It would make a good act. We can pull people up from the audience and have them throw a few darts. Whatever they land on, I'll put between two slices of bread and eat as a sandwich."

"Like an egg, tuna, and Jell-O sandwich?" Mario covers his mouth and pretends to gag. When he uncovers his mouth, though, he's smiling. "Not gonna lie, that sounds pretty funny. Nasty, but funny. What if you throw up onstage?"

I wave my hand. "I've been preparing for this my whole

life. The trick is to swallow with minimum chewing. Less time on the taste buds."

Mario tosses a hacky sack into the air. "So, what do you need me for?"

"I was thinking you could be the assistant. Grab people from the audience, help them know where to stand to throw the arrows. Stuff like that."

Now that I'm saying it out loud, I feel bad that Mario doesn't get to do anything cool. He doesn't look too upset, though. "I guess that'd be easy," he says.

I hang up the dartboard in its usual spot on the wall and throw a dart. It rips through the "garlic" section. "Obviously this is just a prototype. We'll use this dartboard, but I'll get thicker paper and cut it out better."

"Maybe you could put pictures of the foods along with the words," Mario says.

"I like that."

I grab my laptop, and Mario and I search for pictures of pickles, eggs, garlic, dog food, tuna, Spam, Jell-O, spinach, cauliflower, and syrup. We save the best images on a shared Google Doc.

"What do you think of the foods I chose? Are they bad enough?"

Mario rubs his chin. "I think you could add something spicy. Like jalapeños."

"Oh, that's good."

"Or even something that's not technically edible, but that wouldn't kill you. Like . . . I don't know . . . grass."

"That's genius!" I could do grass. In fact, I'm pretty sure I ate grass when I was a kid, just for kicks. It could be a super-tiny section that everyone tries to aim for.

"What else you got?"

He looks at the corner of my room and scrunches his lips. "I don't know. Maybe I could do a hacky sack trick each time before you eat something."

This kid will not drop the hacky sack thing. Every time he mentions it, my chest tightens a little with guilt. "I don't know if we'd have time for that . . . We get two minutes tops."

"I could ask the teachers in charge for a thirty-second extension."

"I'll tell you what. You can kick the hacky sack at the board for the last round, and whatever it hits, I'll add on to the sandwich combo."

He tosses around his sweatshirt strings. "Yeah, okay."

"You can even do a little trick before you kick it if you want." I'm feeling generous.

He perks up a little. "I know exactly which one."

Our doorbell rings and Mario looks at his watch. "That's probably my mom. She needed me home by noon to watch my little sisters."

"Already? That went by so fast."

"Yeah. It stinks. I always get stuck babysitting."

I hand Mario back his hacky sack and then stand to hang my darts on the magnetic section of the dartboard. "You should come over after school sometime next week. Maybe we could put a hacky sack video on MyTube to tease for the tryouts."

His eyes light up. "That'd be fun! I'll have to ask my mom, though. She doesn't like me hanging out on weekdays, but sometimes she makes exceptions if I do work around the house."

His mom sounds like one tough cookie.

We walk toward the doorway to find our moms chatting it up like they've been best friends forever. We hang around the kitchen for a few minutes, tossing avocados around until Mario's mom calls for him to leave. Then I go back to my room and snap a picture of the "pickles" section of the dartboard. I upload it to my MyTube story captioned with a winking emoji. That should get people curious. Especially Zane, since I know he hates pickles. (Should have been a red flag.)

I flop backward onto my bed. Maybe I could include dirt instead of grass. Oh, or worms! There's a whole world of potential.

I almost text Mario but stop when I remember that the message would go straight to his mom. I'm sure she'd be disturbed if she got a random text reading, "What about worms?"

It's definitely inconvenient that he doesn't have a phone, but I still think he could make a good friend.

Not that I'm getting my hopes up.

8

Marshmallow Bribery

Monday, I have lunch detention. I almost forget until Ms. Campbell hands me the green slip near the end of class. She doesn't even bother explaining what to do with it. She probably figures I already know. And she's right. I've never gotten lunch detention from her specifically, but this is my fifth one of the school year, which isn't bad considering school ends in about a month.

My great-grandpa Vance told me that when he was growing up, whenever a kid threw a spitball in class, or didn't do their homework or whatever, the teacher would make them wear this white pointy hat that said "Dunce" on it. (*Dunce*, by the way, means "a stupid person." The dictionary said it, not me.) Anyway, once they put the hat on, they had to stand in the corner facing the wall for the rest of the lesson so everyone would know how dumb they were.

Lunch detention is the modern version of the dunce cap. You have to sit at a table facing the back wall of the cafeteria. Some people call it the Table of Shame. A teacher watches over you as you eat in silence and listen to everyone having fun and talking behind your back—literally.

My school must have missed the memo about cruel and unusual punishments being illegal.

As annoying as it is to eat in silence, this was the best day I could've gotten lunch detention since I'm not sure who I'd sit with otherwise. I obviously can't sit with Zane and his friends anymore. Now that I hung out with Mario, I could sit with him, but I don't know if starting today would be too much Jack too soon. I'd probably end up eating with this group of guys I use as a backup when I don't know where else to go. They can be fun, like that time we got in trouble for spitting milk through our teeth, but other times they'll talk about boring stuff like girls or deodorant brands.

Walking into the cafeteria feels like walking into an oven: it's hot and smells like burnt pizza crust. I hand my green slip to the detention monitor. Today we have Mr. Cooley, part-time social studies teacher, part-time gym coach. He tells me to grab my food as he writes my name down on his clipboard. Usually detention monitors take attendance on their tablets, but I heard Mr. Cooley broke his last two by sitting on them, so Principal Duncan took away his tablet privileges.

Cooley's not too bad. He was the monitor for my first lunch detention and spent half the time traveling to and from the vending machine, so I got to talk to the other people at the Table of Shame. This time, though, I don't want to talk to the other people. Because at least one of them is going to be . . .

"Zane," I mutter as he walks into the cafeteria. He's all decked out in track gear, even though track season ended last week.

I walk over to the pizza line, hoping Zane doesn't stand right behind me. Luckily, he brought his own lunch. He sits at the detention table and sets his paper bag down. Another kid dressed in black walks in and sits next to him. It's Axel, who gets detention even more than I do, though his are usually for ditching class instead of for talking. Axel's the type who tries to sleep throughout the whole period. When he's not etching things into his desk, that is.

The girl in front of me in line has on an orange-striped shirt and a yellow crocheted hat. Tasha. She turns around and gives me a half smile, but she doesn't say anything. I give her a weird half smile back and say, " 'Sup?"

She shrugs. "Just getting lunch." It's funny because "What's up?" is something you don't usually expect people to answer. Tasha's arms are at her sides and she's still facing me. I remember how Mr. Busby talked about reading people's body language, and I think hers is saying that she wants to talk.

"Nice hat."

"Thanks." She touches the top of her head like she needs to feel the hat to remember which one it is. "Made it myself."

If I knew her better, I might snatch her hat and put it on. But considering her head is shaved and I'm still not sure why, that's most likely a terrible idea. Besides, she seems too serious for stuff like that.

The truth is, I'm pretty awful at talking to quiet people.

I bop my head a couple of times. "So, what are you planning on eating this fine afternoon?"

She glances at the menu scrawled on a large whiteboard by the lunch window. "Hamburger and fries, I guess."

"Be careful with those French fries. They're dangerous."

"Huh?"

"My brother stuck one up his nose last year. We had to call the ambulance and everything."

She snorts out a laugh, which surprises me, in a good way. Maybe she's not as serious as I thought. "I'll try to resist the temptation. Man, little kids do the weirdest things."

"Oh, he's eleven."

"Eleven? Yikes."

"Yikes indeed."

Better not to mention I stuck a fry in my nose first. In typical fashion, Josh copied me.

The conversation has come to a standstill, so I pull out my phone and start playing this game where you have to touch the exact center of a bull's-eye as fast as you can. If that sounds stupid to you, it's because it is. But it's strangely addicting.

When it's my turn, I grab my pizza, juice box, cookie, and grape bunch. I sit at the far end of the Table of Shame to put as much distance as possible between Zane and me. I don't look up but speak loudly enough so that he can hear. "Got your training pants on, I see. Try not to have an accident."

Zane scoffs in return.

I know I said I didn't want to talk to him, but I can never resist a training-pants joke.

"Stay quiet," says Mr. Cooley. He's got a Pop-Tart in one hand and balances a Coke on his clipboard with the other. Only teachers are allowed to drink soda at this school, which is so unfair. They've got an exclusive vending machine in the teachers' lounge that I've never managed to break into. They keep that place under lock and key.

I stick my gum under the table and take a big bite of the crunchy pizza. Everyone always bashes cafeteria food, but I'm a fan. Not as good as Dad's homemade pizza, but pizza is pizza. I only wish they served larger slices. I wonder what

Axel's got in his lunch bag and if he'd be willing to share. I'd ask, but he's got his head down, so I can only assume he's sleeping.

Instead I munch on my pizza and read over the posters on the white cinder-block wall. I wonder if Ms. Campbell would let me count this on that reading-log thing I never turn in.

My school must be trying to win the world record for largest collection of inspirational cat posters, because ninety percent of the wall posters have pictures of cats doing random things next to a cheesy quote:

A gray kitten dangling from a branch: "Hang in there!"

A fluffy cat frolicking through a field of flowers: "Enjoy this moment."

A cat and dog posed next to a puzzle: "Work together."

A grumpy black cat: "Anger is one letter short of danger."

"Yeow!" Mr. Cooley's soda can wobbles on his clipboard before it clangs to the floor. The pop gushes into a large brown puddle. Mr. Cooley drops his clipboard and Pop-Tart and snatches the can. "Blast it," he mutters, shaking off his now-wet shoes. Axel pokes his head up from his arms, and Zane snickers under his breath. No one except us three seems to have noticed what happened.

"I gotta grab something to clean this up," Mr. Cooley says. "Don't let anyone walk through this puddle, got it?" We nod.

Once Mr. Cooley's gone, Axel grabs a sandwich out of his lunch bag. It looks like that's all he's got, so I guess I won't ask him to share.

"So, what's the deal with pickles?" Axel asks.

It takes a moment to register. "Oh, like on my MyTube story?"

"Yeah. Does it have to do with the talent show?"

I throw Zane a smug look, hoping he's taking note that even I-don't-care-about-anything Axel is curious about my talent show act.

"Yep," I say. "It's gonna be sweet."

Axel shakes his hair out of his eyes. "Are you gonna, like, juggle pickles or something?"

"Nah. Way better."

Zane pops open his bag of Takis and looks at Axel. "Don't believe it. He doesn't have a plan. He doesn't even have a partner."

I have the sudden urge to snatch those Takis and dump them all over Zane's head. Or eat them, since I'd hate to waste perfectly good food. "First of all, I do have a plan, and it's gonna be Paxton Poker quality."

"Ha!" Zane says. "Paxton Poker? Yeah, right."

Zane knows and respects the Poker. Our mutual love of him was one of the main reasons we became friends. One time, we tried to recreate his Jell-O-in-the-bathtub challenge, but Mom made us drain it when she realized what was going on. Zane didn't even offer to help me scrub the stains.

"Second of all," I say, "I do have a partner. I found him the same day you dropped out." I shrug like it was the easiest thing in the world to replace him. And honestly, it kind of was. I don't miss Zane at all. The good thing about not being able to keep a friend is that you don't get attached, kind of like how it's less sad when your goldfish dies after a few weeks than when your dog dies after five years.

Zane was nothing but a goldfish to me.

"Who's your partner?" Axel asks me. He holds his hand out to ask Zane for Takis, but Zane pretends not to notice.

I swallow a bite of pizza. "Mario."

"Never heard of him," Axel says.

"He's cool."

Zane crinkles his empty Taki bag back into his lunch sack. "I know that kid. He's not that cool."

Now he's crossed a line. Why does Zane think he gets to decide who's cool and who's not at this school?

"What do you know about cool?" I say loudly.

"Pipe down," Mr. Cooley says as he walks back into the cafeteria. He takes the white towel off his shoulder and spreads it over the Coke spill. The towel turns light brown, and then gets darker and darker until it's sopping wet. I can feel anger seeping into me the same way. I clench my teeth and stare at the black-cat poster in front of my face.

I need to get away from this table before I start throwing my grapes at Zane. The clock says there's five minutes left of lunch. For once, I'm glad we only get twenty-five minutes to eat.

"Hey, Cooley," I say. "Since we protected the puddle, can you let us off the hook five minutes early?" He snorts and shakes his head.

He dropped his Pop-Tart earlier. I bet he's hungry.

"Come on, I'll give you my grapes. And . . ." I dig my marshmallow bag out of my pocket and examine it. "About twenty mini marshmallows."

Cooley eyes the marshmallows and scrunches his lips. He comes close and glances over his shoulder before taking the bag.

"Keep this under wraps, or I won't cut you a deal again." He pops a marshmallow into his mouth and motions toward the other tables with his chin. "Go on."

Zane shoots out of his seat to join his buddies. Axel stays put and lays his head back down. I could stay and talk to him, but I really need to find Mario and ask when he can come over this week. It's been a while since I posted a long video on MyTube, and last night, I thought of an idea that's pure gold. It's destined for massive view count.

I scan the cafeteria and spot Mario sitting with Perry at a table in the corner. Do they always sit together? They seem so different. Perry's nice, but he's always snort-laughing at the teacher's bad jokes, and he's got video-game characters plastered all over his binders and locker. Once, I even heard him discussing the benefits of fiber supplements with his desk partner. At least he seems smart. Sometimes I think I'd rather be smart and nerdy than dumb and funny. Too bad I can't be smart and cool, like Jacob. Lucky firstborns.

"Later, Axel." I toss him my cookie before I leave to talk to Mario. "And don't listen to what Zane said. The talent show won't disappoint. Spread the word."

Zane would love to make people think I'm not funny. He knows it's the only thing I have going for me. This talent show act has to leave no doubt: I *am* the Funny Guy, and no one—not even Zane Peterson—can take that away.

9

Slappin' Awesome

On Tuesday after school, Mom picks up Mario and me in our blue minivan. Mario invited Perry too, but he had some online gaming competition he couldn't miss. Good thing, too, because what I have planned for today is kind of a two-person thing. Although I guess we could have used an extra cameraman.

I pull the handle of the car door. We wait as it slides open like an obnoxiously slow elevator. "Perry's car is just like this," Mario observes.

I duck my head and follow him inside. "Oh yeah? Not surprised. Only the cool kids ride these babies. They've got extra cup holders and everything."

"Hello, boys," Mom says. She looks extra awake since she didn't have to work yesterday. Her hair is coiled up in a dark bun, and she's wearing more makeup than usual.

I buckle my seat belt. "So, are you and Perry, like, best friends or something?" They didn't seem to talk to each other much when I stopped by their lunch table yesterday.

Mario looks down. "We've known each other since we were little, so . . . I guess?"

Mom interrupts. "You know, Mario, your mother is the nicest lady. I really enjoyed talking to her when she came to pick you up the other day. On Saturday, we ran into each other at the grocery store. We were both in the vitamin aisle! She was grabbing calcium pills and I was picking up Flintstone vitamins for Jack. He doesn't eat nearly enough vegetables."

Ugh. It's like she's intentionally trying to embarrass me in front of my new friend.

Mario nudges me. "Flintstone vitamins, huh?"

"Who *doesn't* eat Flintstone vitamins? They're retro."

Our moms being buddy-buddy is a recipe for embarrassment, but it also means Mario is allowed to come over more often. Having a talkative mom has its perks.

I wonder if Mario's mom is friends with Perry's mom too.

"Hey, you haven't told Perry about the dartboard, have you?"

Mario shakes his head. "Nuh-uh. I knew you didn't want anyone knowing about it."

"Good. It has to be a surprise."

"So," Mario says, drumming his fingers on the window. "What's this amaaaazing video you wanted to make today?"

I put my finger to my lips and motion to my mom. She's bopping her head to the radio, so I don't think she heard him.

"We're gonna practice hacky sack!" I say loudly, and then I whisper, "You'll see."

When we're back home and safe in my room, I hop onto my couch and take out my phone. "I wanna show you this clip of a soap opera I was watching with my grandma the other day. Uh . . . I mean, I saw part of it by accident. I wasn't, like, watching it *with* her."

Mario laughs and sits next to me. "You love soap operas. Admit it."

"We visit my grandma every Sunday! She always has them on!"

"I didn't even know soap operas were still a thing."

"They're a thing in Grammy Reynolds's house. They're dying a slow death, though, according to her." I pull up You-Tube and search through my saved videos for the right one. Luckily, someone else uploaded the clip online so I didn't have to.

"We could totally spoof this," I say. "Prepare your eyes, because I don't know if they can handle the awesomeness."

I press Play. The video isn't the best quality since whoever uploaded it to YouTube recorded with their phone, so I make sure the volume is all the way up.

Scene: Small-town diner. Rain pours on the other side of the window. A woman in a blue dress sits at a booth and checks her watch.

Man in a fedora *(bursting into the diner, sopping wet):* Suzanne! I'm sorry I'm late. I . . . I need to tell you something.

Woman *(sneering):* It's too late, Fabio. I know where you've been. I know what you've done.

Man *(grabbing his chest):* You're not talking about—

Woman *(rising from her seat):* Yes. Linda. The beautiful Linda. *(Cackles.)* You think I didn't know that you two were secretly engaged? And all this while trying to woo me?!

Man: I can explain.

Woman: Explain it to the ketchup!

Then she grabs the red bottle off the table and squirts it at him like she's wielding a water gun. She gets his shirt, his face, even his dorky fedora. The funniest part is that he doesn't even try to run away—the acting is that bad. He just pulls a horrified face and flails his arms and shouts, "I shouldn't have trusted you!" before he wipes the red goop out of his eyes.

When the video ends, Mario's cracking up as loud as I am. I'm glad he's able to appreciate the beauty of terrible scripting.

"So, what are you thinking?" Mario says. "You wanna

squirt ketchup at each other? Because my mom would freak if I stained this shirt."

"I come prepared." I walk over to my closet and pull a large rain poncho off the top shelf. "I got this at Disneyland last summer. I knew it would come in handy one day."

"Oh, man. I guess that works. So yes to the ketchup fight? Wouldn't we need two ponchos?"

"Only one of us needs to get dirty if we follow their script. I was thinking we could use the same lines, but substitute different foods in place of ketchup. Then we could figure out the best food to throw at someone if you're mad."

"You and food, man."

"It's a passion."

"What food do you have?"

"There are tons of leftovers in the fridge." I open my bedroom door. "Let's go see."

We walk down the hall and wait outside the kitchen for Jacob to finish digging through the pantry. He finds what he's looking for—rice cakes, no shocker—and passes us as he returns to his room *with* the food. Mom doesn't like us eating in our bedrooms (hence the minifridge denial). I almost want to tell on Jacob, but then I remember I'm about to bring food into my room too. Just not to snack on.

Now that the kitchen is empty, we hurry inside and open the fridge. The first thing I see is leftover homemade pizza.

"We don't wanna take something that's too good," I say. "We want something no one will care about."

"Yeah," says Mario. "Like, I hate pie-in-the-face pranks. It's such a waste of pie."

"Exactly! I hate those too!" Man, we are so much alike.

We've only gathered three items when we hear my mom coming down the hall.

"Three's good enough!" I shout-whisper. "Run!"

We dart to my room, arms loaded, and shut ourselves in before Mom reaches the kitchen.

Mario lets out a breath and sets his food item on my desk. "Close call. You don't think your mom will ban me from coming over if she finds out about this, do you?"

"Nah. She's used to stuff like this." My brothers and I have done way worse, especially when we were younger and hung out more. Once, we set up a mud-pie factory in Josh's room. Mom loves telling that story to our aunts and uncles, so it couldn't have made her that mad.

Mario chooses to be the fedora man. I don't have a fedora, so he improvises by turning his baseball cap to the side. Since I'm playing the girl, I wrap a giant blue scarf around my chest so it looks like a dress over my normal shirt.

"It'd be better if you had a wig," Mario says. "What about that mop in your pantry?"

"A mop?"

"Yeah. It was yellow, like the blonde in the soap opera. You could put the mop head on your head."

I slap Mario's back. "The genius strikes again!"

This time, I sneak into the kitchen alone and return in less than thirty seconds with the mop. I take the head off the long handle and place it over my head, tucking the strings behind my ears the best I can. It smells like wet dog, and we don't even have a dog. I'll need a good shower tonight, but it will be worth it.

"Let's do this thing," I say.

"Wait. Won't your mom get mad if you get food all over your floor?"

Again, he has a point, especially since our carpets were cleaned last month. I travel to the kitchen for the third time and grab trash bags to cover the ground. I'm glad Mario thinks ahead, but we're running behind schedule. It's already been a half hour, and his mom is only letting him stay an hour.

Once the floor is all trash-bagged, I reapply my mop hair. "Okay, so we don't have time for any run-throughs. I'll start by explaining to the viewers what we're gonna do, and then we'll prop up my phone to reenact the scene." I hand the phone over and show him how to use it. I have no idea the level of recording amateur I'm working with.

"We need a hand signal to let you know when to press Pause," I say.

"Just scratch your ear."

"Okay, sure." There's no time to think of anything better.

Mario sits on my desk chair, and I take a spot in the center of the couch. He points at me and mouths, "Go."

I clap. "*Heyyy*, Jacksters."

"Pause." Mario puts the phone down. "*Jacksters?*"

"Yeah, I was thinking I need to start calling my fans a nickname. You know, how like Beyoncé fans are the Beyhive."

"I've never heard of that. I don't think that's a thing."

"It's a thing. I promise. Now, no more pauses—we're running low on time."

"Yeah, yeah." He points again.

"So, over the weekend, I . . . uh, I mean my grandma . . . was watching this soap opera called *Weeks in Our Lives*. That is when my eyes first feasted upon *this* clip of cinematic masterpiece." I scratch my ear, and Mario puts the phone down.

"Here's where we'll insert the ketchup clip," I say.

"Should I start again?"

"Yeah."

I place my hand over my heart. "Wasn't that just beautiful? Anyway, this got me and my buddy Mario thinking, what is the best food to throw at someone if you're in a fight? Today . . ." I scratch my ear and tell Mario to get in the shot for the next clip. I record us selfie-style.

"Let's find out!" we both shout.

I stop recording. "And here I can edit it to put cartoon sunglasses over our faces and play rap music in the background."

Mario's eyebrows shoot up. "You know how to do that?"

"Yeah. I've taught myself some editing stuff."

"Impressive."

Next we prop my phone on my dresser to reenact the soap-opera scene. We don't have time to memorize the words perfectly, so I take some liberties.

"Fabio, you scum of the earth!" I say before I splatter him with the first item: mayonnaise. Mario pulls a perfect overly dramatic face as the mayo globs onto his Disney poncho.

"I've been hit!" he yells, crumpling to the floor. I dig my spoon into the jar and fling another glob at him, but it flies across the room and splatters on my bed instead. Looks like I'm washing my sheets tonight.

In the next shot, I smack Mario across the face with waffles, smeared with jelly for good measure (there was a little left in the ketchup bottle). He claps when the waffle hits his cheek as a sound effect, and then stumbles into the wall. "How dare you!"

The third time around, I peel the lid off the large Tupperware container of week-old spaghetti that was crammed into the fridge's back corner. We run through the script, and when it's slapping time, I shout, "Talk to the spaghetti, because the face ain't gonna listen!"

The spaghetti makes a fun smacky sound against the poncho that we don't even have to fake sound effects for. Mario breaks character and laughs, but I try to stay serious. I do another smack across his face, and he gets sauce in his hair.

Mario makes a loud, croaky gasp. "Revenge!" He grabs a fistful of spaghetti from the Tupperware dish and tosses it at me before I can duck. "How dare you?" I say in a Southern accent, despite "Suzanne" never having been Southern before. I somersault away, and my wig falls off. "You ruined my hair!"

Once we've gotten enough footage, I turn the camera off, and we assess the damage. Mario's clothes are clean, but my shirt got stained. A small price to pay for internet stardom.

For the last segment of our video, we sit on the couch to discuss our conclusions.

"All right, guys," I say. "After much debate and consideration, Mario and I have our rankings for best food to slap someone with. In third place, we chose . . ." I drumroll on my lap. "Waffles. Waffles might be satisfying if you had, like, a giant waffle. But normal ones are too small, so you have to get really close to the person you're hitting. It gives them too much time to escape."

Mario explains next. "For second place, we chose mayonnaise. If you can aim for their mouth, it'll be nice and disgusting. Problem is, it's hard to aim well when you're using a spoon." He side-eyes in my direction. "As we all saw."

I take over. "That makes first place . . . spaghetti! Spaghetti is the ideal slapping food because not only does it get your enemy all saucy, but the strands are long enough that you don't have to be too accurate with your aim."

"Yeah," Mario adds. "Who has time to calculate distance when they're in a fit of rage?"

"Throwin' out the big words, Dr. Mario." I high-five him. "So the verdict is in, Jacksters. If you're ever mad at someone, you should slap them with spaghetti!"

The world is truly a better place now that we all know.

I put my mop hair back on for the last line—my signature phrase I use to sign off on all my videos:

"Thanks for watching, and gotta run."

10

A Brutal Farewell

The video's a hit. The next day at school, I'll be walking down the halls and random people will call out stuff like, "You should do a food slap, part two!" or, "Hey, use bacon next!" Every time someone mentions the video, I reply with, "It was slappin' awesome, right?" *Fish sticks* hasn't been catching on, but *slappin' awesome* has potential.

At lunch, I sit with Mario and Perry without even worrying whether Mario would think it was weird. I guess that's a sign we're really friends now. Perry says a guy in his class started playing the video when the teacher went to the bathroom, and everyone gathered around his desk to watch it. Mario's proud that people have been recognizing him and calling him Fabio, which he much prefers to Mario Kart. We're just a few hundred hits away from beating the view count of my T-rexing video. Take that, Zane!

Mario lends me a hacky sack, so after school, I practice a little in my room. The tryouts are tomorrow, and I'm hoping to pin down a simple trick I can do other than just toss the sack to Mario. Even though Mario's amazing at hacky sack, he's all jittery because he's never performed before. We're planning on running through our routine in the hall ten minutes before tryouts.

After fifteen minutes and only minimal ceiling damage, I'm able to kick the hacky sack with my right foot, kick it with my knee, and catch it in my hand. That's good enough. I head to the kitchen to reward myself with a snack.

I grab a frozen burrito and pop it into the microwave. While I'm waiting, I lean against the counter and read through more of the comments on our video, which we titled "SLAP OPERA!!" Most of the comments are people tagging friends. Others ask for a follow-up video, so I'll have to see if Mario is down for that. I'd totally play Fabio next time.

A few people mention me scratching my ear before every scene cut, and one person even sends a link for itching cream. Others give me flak about the Transformers posters on my wall, which I don't get. Transformers are awesome.

Maybe I should take my posters down for our next video.

Or better, I could go over-the-top and plaster dozens of giant Transformers posters all over, just to show them I don't care.

Only a few people are really negative. They say stuff like, "This is sooooo dumb. I just wasted eight minutes of my life!"

But at least we got them to waste it.

The microwave beeps, and I take out my burrito. I'm wrapping it in a paper towel when Mom walks into the kitchen.

"Jack, I got an email from Mario's mother. She's very concerned." Mom leans her elbows on the kitchen island. "She sent me a link to the video you boys made the other day. She'd like you to take it down."

Fat chance! How did Mario's mom even find out about this? And why does she care?

I swallow a bite of burrito. "No way. It's my best video yet. What's the big deal?"

Mom sighs. "I'm not going to lie, Jack. I thought the video was harmless. At least you boys cleaned up after yourselves. But I'm used to these shenanigans. Nydia wants to protect her son's online image."

"Online image?" I pull a face.

"Yeah. Like, what if a future employer saw this?"

I take another bite. "Then they'd obviously hire us in a heartbeat."

"Well, it might not be a big deal to you, but some people are more sensitive about these things than others."

I shrug. "Why does she care so much anyway? She's always up in Mario's business."

"Because she's a parent and she wants the best for her child. I'm starting to think I need to be more 'up in your business' too."

This conversation had better not be headed where I think it's headed.

Mom takes out her phone. "I've been reading through the comments on this video, and some of them are really rude."

"I just ignore those. You're always going to get trolls."

"And the words some of these kids use! Didn't their mothers ever teach them to watch their language?"

I roll my eyes behind her back. If she thinks *these* comments are bad, she should walk down the hallway at my school.

The front door opens and shuts. "I'm home," Dad calls.

Great. If Dad gets involved, things will not go well. He grumbles about the subject of MyTube every time it comes up. He thinks we should all live in the dark ages and go fishing every weekend and play board games every night.

Dad walks into the kitchen, still wearing his white chef's outfit, and puts his arm around Mom's waist. "Remember how the kids used to come running whenever I came home, hon?" He chuckles quietly.

I stuff the rest of the burrito into my mouth and try to leave before this turns into a "discussion about phone privileges" with both my parents.

"Stop!" Mom calls before I can escape. *Fish sticks.*

She makes me come back and listen as she rehashes the whole video drama to Dad, who shakes his head and grunts periodically. When she finishes, they force me to delete the video in front of them, which makes me so mad, I want to punch a hole in the wall.

"This is so stupid!" I growl as I hit delete. Who knows how much that video could have grown? And now it's gone. I curl my fists so tightly that my nails dig into my palms.

"You're being ridiculous," Dad says. He turns to Mom. "Remind me why he even has a phone. A thirteen-year-old is clearly not mature enough to handle it."

"We didn't want him to feel left out." She rubs her forehead. "We wanted him to be able to communicate with us."

"Yeah, but he doesn't need one with the internet or all the fancy gadgets."

"You mean apps," I say. "And you kind of do unless you want to be a social outcast."

That's not totally true. Mario doesn't seem like an outcast. But I won't take it back, because the point seems to work well with Mom.

Dad throws up his hands. "I say we take it away." He can't be serious.

Mom looks at me like I'm a wounded puppy. She opens her mouth, closes it, and then opens it again. "Maybe it wouldn't hurt to have a little break."

"Wha-what?" I sputter. "I didn't even do anything wrong!"

"You're glued to your phone all the time," Mom says. "We can't get through a meal without you checking it. We never spend time as a family anymore."

"That's not my fault!" I grip the side of the counter. "Jacob's always doing homework, and Josh is always with his friends. Dad's on his phone all the time too, and *you're* always tired from work."

Dad's voice gets stern. "Don't use that tone with your mother. She sacrifices everything for you boys."

"Honey, it's fine." Mom touches Dad's arm. "Jack's just voicing his concern, and you know what? He's right."

That was unexpected. I loosen my grip on the counter.

"You're right," she repeats, looking at me with worn-out eyes. "We *all* need to work on making more time for each other."

Dad's face softens and he nods slowly.

"Your father and I will think about how *we* can improve. As for you, let's start with a little technology fast." She holds out her palm.

I clutch my phone in my pocket. "What about my My-Tube? I have people counting on me to put up videos."

"They'll survive," Mom says.

"What if there's an emergency? What if I'm kidnapped?"

Mom gives Dad a wary look, but he stays firm. "We'll get you a phone that can only make calls in the meantime. Now, please don't make us ask again."

I drop the phone into Mom's hand and glare at the tile. They'd better not get me one of those dinosaur phones you see at the grocery store. I'd rather be caught dead than using one of those barfblocks. I speak through clenched teeth. "When do I get it back?"

Dad crosses his arms. "I want to see your grades improve, as well as your attitude."

"I can't just magically start getting better grades."

"When you put your mind to something, you really excel," Mom says. "You just need to apply yourself."

They expect me to be smart like Jacob. Why can't they understand that that's just not who I am? I breathe in through my nose. "So if I get good grades and behave and stuff, then I can get my phone back?"

Mom puts her hand on my shoulder to try to soften me up, but it doesn't work. "You'll get it back. In the meantime, try to enjoy the phone break. You may find you don't need it as much as you thought you did."

She doesn't get it. MyTube is the one thing I'm good at. It's where I can be myself and have people appreciate me for who I am. Why do they have to take that away from me? It's like they want to control every part of my life.

101

And what about the talent show in two weeks? I won't be able to record and post my act. I worked hard making the food dartboard, finding a partner, building up suspense around school. I need my phone back before then, or all that work was for nothing.

11

Going Solo

I pass by Mario's locker before school the next day. Part of me wants to yell at him for telling his mom about the video, but I have no idea if it's his fault. When he sees me, his eyes quickly dart away, like he's considering running. Sign of guilt, if you ask me.

I lean against the locker next to his. "So, my mom got an interesting email yesterday."

He scratches the back of his head. "Dude. I am so sorry. One of her friends sent the video to her. I guess her son follows you. I'm grounded for a week, starting today."

Believable excuse, and he looks like he feels bad. I guess

I can't be mad at him. It's not his fault that the woman who birthed him is this way.

"A week just for making a video? Geesh. At least you'll be ungrounded right in time for the talent show."

"About that." He shuts his locker and stares at the ground. "I would get in so much trouble if we signed up to do hacky sack and then switched to something else. Plus, my mom wouldn't want the video to be online. I don't get the big deal, but she's . . . weird, I guess."

Another one bites the dust. That terrible eighties song my dad listens to starts playing in my head. Now I'm going to have to go partner searching all over again. I should have known this friendship with Mario was too good to be true.

I swallow the big lump in my throat. "Yeah, man. You're right."

"I can still try out with you after school if you want. Then you can just find someone else to help you with the final performance."

That sounds like a bad idea. If his mom found out he did the tryouts and not the performance, she'd think I kicked her precious baby out of my act. She'd tattle to Mom and I could lose even more privileges. I have to go solo.

"Don't worry about it. I'll figure something out."

"But tryouts are after school. What will you do?"

"I'll think of something." I poke my finger into the locker

door vents. "I'm bummed that you can't do the show any-more."

"Yeah. Me too."

But he doesn't look that bummed. Something inside me isn't convinced that doing the show was ever that impor-tant to him. He could have fought harder to make his mom understand, or even risked getting in trouble to do it with me. He gave up too easily.

Maybe he's relieved he's grounded. Now he doesn't have to do the show *and* he doesn't have to hang out with me for a week. It's just like with Zane; he probably thinks I'm not worth the trouble. I know how this goes.

That's why at lunch, I don't bother sitting with Mario and Perry. They've been friends since they were little. I shouldn't bother trying to butt in on something like that. Instead I sit with the milk-spitter dudes. It goes all right, and they don't even talk about brands of deodorant this time. I almost ask one of them to do the tryouts, but if things turn out badly like they did with Mario and Zane, then I'd have to find a new fallback crew. I'd rather ask someone who I never have to see again if things don't work out.

Guess I'm going back to speed friendshipping tomorrow. But first, I have to face the tryouts alone. I don't know if I'll end up doing the final show, but I need to get through try-outs just in case.

Luckily, I have one talent I'm always able to pull out of my hat when needed.

There are only about fifteen kids in the auditorium after school. The fewer the better. I don't need a big crowd viewing my talent since it will be decent at best. I take a squishy chair in the second row and swivel the seat so my knees are up to my chest. These chairs are way comfier than the classroom ones.

Ms. Campbell is one of the teachers in charge of the tryouts. Earlier today, I told her the song I wanted to sing so she could download a ninety-second clip of it for me. She walks onstage and speaks into the microphone. "All right, everyone, we're ready to start! Now, these aren't auditions so much as a run-through, so don't be nervous. We just have to approve your act and make sure it's school appropriate. If it's not, we can work with you." She looks at her clipboard. "We'll call you up in alphabetical order by last name."

A few seats down from me, Brielle closes her eyes and takes deep breaths in and out. I've seen clips of her dancing on MyTube, and she's great, so I don't get why she's nervous. I've never gotten stage fright myself. If things go wrong, I'm good at improvising. Like, when I was the turkey in the third-grade Thanksgiving play, I forgot my lines, so I just ran around gobbling. And during my first (and only) piano recital, when I botched the notes halfway through, I started pounding on random keys with dramatic hand motions. Everyone thought it was funny (except for my teacher), and it wasn't a big deal.

This won't be a big deal, either. I just want to get it over with. No act is ever as funny without a sidekick.

Ms. Campbell sits next to a couple of other teachers at the judges' table and starts calling up the students. There's a violinist, a karate girl, and a singer who belts the last note of "Over the Rainbow" so loud, I swear I hear the clock glass crack. One Hula-Hooper's background music has some bad words in it, so Ms. Campbell takes her aside to ask her to pick a new song. Brielle goes right before me and does perfectly, naturally. She wears a leotard with a flowy white skirt and tights, and dances to some classical song that sounds like it's a billion years old.

"Jack Reynolds," Ms. Campbell says after Brielle finishes, and everyone in the auditorium starts to whisper. I hope they don't have their hopes up. I've only told Zane and Mario that this is just a decoy act because I didn't want word getting out to the teachers. As the whispering gets louder, I realize I have to play things up at least a little because everyone's obviously expecting some entertainment.

My new goal is to be louder than "Over the Rainbow" girl. Gotta get that soft palate up.

I walk onstage and grab the mic off its stand. I point to Ms. Campbell and wink. "You know what to do."

She shakes her head, smiling, and then plays the music: the *Pokémon* theme song. A classic.

I pump my shoulders up and down to the beat while shuffling around the stage, and then shout-sing the first line like the world's wackiest karaoke star.

People whoop and dance and pull out their phones to record. Somehow, I didn't think about how people might record this. I spike up my energy.

When my favorite line comes up, I throw myself on my knees and toss my head back, singing. I slap the floor before

OHHHH, YOU'RE MY BEST FRIEND, IN A WORLD WE MUST DEFEND!

getting up. Then I start throwing pretend Poké Balls and somersaulting across the stage, which isn't easy to do while singing.

At the end of my act, I'm totally out of breath, but the applause is louder than it was for any of the other acts. I take a sweeping bow twice in a row. "I didn't get kicked out of choir for nothing!" I say into the mic. "I was making people jealous!" Everyone laughs at that, since they know I got kicked out because Ms. Liverston hated me.

"Thank you for your very . . . *expressive* act," Ms. Campbell says from the judges' table. "As long as you don't mention getting kicked out of choir, you're signed off to perform."

"Dealio," I say, hopping off the stage. That performance didn't turn out so bad after all. I wonder if anyone livestreamed it, or if they're planning on posting it later. I hate how I can't see the reactions. If MyTube had a web version, I might be able to look it up on my laptop, but you can only access it through the app.

There are only two acts left after mine. While the next performer is playing her turbo-speed song on the piano, the guy in front of me turns around. His name is Michael Lee, and he played the violin for his act. I talked to him a little at speed friendshipping.

"That was awesome." He adjusts his wire-framed glasses. "Weren't you going to do something with Zane, though?"

"Nah. Long story."

I notice the phone in his hand. I wonder . . . "Hey, could I borrow your phone?"

He draws his hand back. "For what?"

"I just have to check something." I plead with my eyes. "Can I use it for, like, five minutes?"

"That long?"

I pull my secret weapon out of my back pocket. "I'll give you some marshmallows."

He sighs, and then unlocks his phone. "Fine."

I dig a handful of marshmallows out of the bag and drop them in his palm. These have really been coming in handy lately.

Michael gives me the phone, and it fits perfectly in my hand. It feels warm and inviting, like reuniting with a long-lost friend. I tap on the MyTube icon and log into my account with my password, *hedgehogsrcool*. My heart jolts when I see the number of notifications piled up! How am I gonna check all of these in five minutes?

I scan through the notifications: lots of likes and comments on my videos and stories. My main goal was to see if my Pokémon performance is on here yet. I tap through the circles at the top of my feed, but I don't see it. I do see a video that Zane posted of himself backflipping off a wall. "Vote for Zane," he says at the end. Puh-lease. Would people really vote for him just because of that?

Michael's still happily munching on marshmallows, so I scroll through the main feed, hoping to see my face pop up.

Instead I see a post from the account StayLovelyWith-Brielle. In the photo, she's doing stretches and wearing her white leotard. "Talent show tryouts today!" the caption says. I check the comments to see if anyone asked about my act.

Most people put heart-eye emojis, or some variation of "You're so pretty!" But one comment near the bottom surprises me.

"Great, we get to watch Brielle show off again," says an account that doesn't have a profile photo, just an anonymous purple icon.

"Snoozefest," another account replies.

I've come across my fair share of meanness on MyTube, but this is pretty bad. The harshest comments are always the ones that have some truth to them.

Down the aisle, Brielle stares into her pink leather purse, sneakily scrolling through her phone, and for the first time, I feel sorry for her. I wonder if she deals with this kind of stuff a lot.

I check out another one of her posts and see a similar comment: "Brielle is soooo pretty. Pretty BORING."

It all makes sense now. At speed friendshipping, Brielle

seemed bothered when I said she never got in trouble. Then she asked if I thought she was boring. This has obviously been on her mind for a while.

If she's wanting to change her image, I think I know how we can help each other.

12

Let's Make a Deal

The *Pokémon* theme song wiggles its way into everyone's heads and refuses to leave. On Friday, people are singing it in the halls or whistling it during class. We even got Ms. Campbell to play it during the ten minutes of free time she gives us every Friday. People seemed to like my talent, so if worse comes to worst and I can't find a partner, I could sing another song. Repeating myself isn't ideal, though. It's not up to my standard.

Going into speed friendshipping today, I have two goals: (1) Find another talent show partner and (2) convince Brielle to feature me on her MyTube. Even though I'm not actively using my own account, I can still show up on other people's. Mom created her own MyTube to snoop on me, but since she's not friends with Brielle, she wouldn't see the tag.

In the drama room, the chairs are set up the same way as last Friday, with two rows facing each other. This time, however, there are no Popsicle sticks and no desks between the chairs. Just empty space.

Most of the people from last time are back, like Michael Lee, Larissa the weasel owner, Mei-ling, Tasha, Mario, Perry, and Brielle. I still don't get why she comes, but I'm glad she's here, since we need to talk. About ten extra people showed up who weren't here last time, including Axel, which surprises me. He doesn't seem like the type of kid who'd wanna join an after-school program. He doesn't even show up to class half the time.

Luckily, Principal Duncan is gone today. I definitely won't miss him scowling at me. Instead Mr. Busby stands next to a tall, thin lady whose hair poofs up in the back. Her brown lipstick against her white skin makes it look like she just ate a chocolate bar. She walks over to Tasha and says, "Hey, you! Long time no see," before crouching down to chat with her. I wonder how they know each other.

Mr. Busby nods at me. "Glad to see you here again, Jack." He straightens his purple skinny tie over his black shirt and walks in front of the "You belong here" phrase on the whiteboard. "Take your seats."

It'd be too obvious I want something if I paired up with Brielle immediately, so I sit a couple of seats down on the opposite side of her. Mario and Perry are in the green-chair row with me, so I won't get paired with either of them, thank goodness. Mario and I have started the fade-out phase of our friendship, and it's always awkward to make small talk with someone you used to hang out with. He hasn't said anything to me since this morning, so I think we're both moving on.

Mr. Busby motions down the center of the rows. "You may have noticed there are no Popsicle sticks today. That's because I think you guys are creative enough to come up with your own questions."

I sit cross-legged on my chair. "It's because you didn't feel like writing more Popsicle-stick questions, isn't it?"

He chuckles. "Okay, that might have been a teeny part of it. But I also believe conversations are more enjoyable when you get to ask what you want to know." He points to a sentence he's written on the top corner of the whiteboard. "'To be interesting, be interested.' That's a quote from Dale Carnegie. He wrote the book *How to Win Friends and Influence People*."

"Win friends?" Michael says. "That sounds like tricking people into liking you."

"It might sound that way. But it's not about manipulating. It's about genuinely being interested in what someone has to say. People love talking about themselves—so let them! Ask your partner about their hobbies, their dreams, their background. Sometimes people will surprise you."

This is getting too touchy-feely for me. "Did you bring pizza?" I ask to lighten the mood.

"Even better. I brought Jolly Ranchers." He holds up the bag, smiling as if they're actually as good as pizza. Psht. I have a billion Jolly Ranchers stocked up from last Halloween. I'm not patient enough for that candy. I end up biting them and they get stuck in my teeth.

I fold my arms. "Doesn't sound like you really *listened* to what I suggested last week."

"I hear your concerns." Mr. Busby sets down the bag. "But like I said, we have budget issues." He claps. "Okay, we're upping the talking time to three minutes. For the first half, those in the green chairs will lead the conversation. And then you'll switch." He clicks a button on his watch. "Start."

The kid in front of me is in my science class, but we never talk. All I know about him is his name is Kevin and he asks to sit in the front every seating change because he has a hard time seeing the board. I'm supposed to lead the conversation, but talking about his eyesight sounds less than thrilling.

I finally come up with, "What's your favorite Pokémon?" mostly because the song's still stuck in my head.

"I don't pay attention to Pokémon," Kevin sneers, like it's oh-so beneath him.

What did Pokémon ever do to you? I almost ask, but it's not worth it to get into a three-minute argument with some dude I barely know. "What's your favorite movie?" I ask instead.

"I don't know. I watch TV more than movies."

This guy can't even answer a question as simple as *What's your favorite movie?* How on earth am I supposed to find *him* interesting?

I stare blankly and almost resort to asking about his eyesight.

"But my favorite TV show is probably *The Great British Bake Off*," he offers. "It's a competitive baking show."

From there, I'm able to ask him about baking, which isn't really my thing, but it gets him talking enough that I mostly have to nod and not think of more questions. I even convince him to bring cookies to speed friendshipping next Friday, which are much better than Jolly Ranchers, so at least something good came of this. When it's his turn to lead, he asks me about my favorite TV show, but I end up telling him about my favorite MyTube channels instead. He doesn't understand the humor of most of Paxton Poker's pranks, but he seems mildly interested in the sword fight with French bread, even though I can't answer his questions about the type of baguettes they used, or whether they were topped with sesame seeds.

My next partner is Michael, who I bribed with marshmallows yesterday. We talk about the tryouts, and he asks me how life is without my phone, which is nice because I get to vent about how terrible and unfair my parents are. I could ask *him* if he wants to join my act since he'll be at the talent show anyway, but something tells me to wait until I'm totally sure I'm choosing the right partner. I have two weeks, so I don't have to rush it.

In fact, it might even be best to ask someone a few days before the show so they have less time to drop out.

Next up is Brielle. She smiles when I take the seat in front of her, almost like she doesn't mind it's me.

"Well, if it isn't our resident chatterbox," I say. "Have you been talking during class lately?"

She rolls her eyes. "Hello, Jack. *Always* a pleasure."

I want to get straight to my proposal, but I'm not sure how to bring it up. It's probably best to soften her up with some flattery.

"Great job at the tryouts, by the way. How long have you been dancing?"

"I've taken classes since I was three." She glances at the woman volunteer pacing down the aisles. "My mom is kind of intense like that." Hers and Mario's both. Lots of intense mothers around these parts.

"Well, it paid off. It was amazing."

"Thanks. I worked hard on it. Though I know it might not have been as . . . exciting as yours."

She's worrying about being exciting again. There's not gonna be a better time to bring up my offer than now.

"Look." I rest my forearms on my knees and lean in. "This might be weird to say, but I saw some jerk on your MyTube saying you're boring and stuck up and stuff like that. I just wanted to let you know that I don't think that's true."

I used to think it was true, although I can't admit it out loud. But for some reason my opinion changed, even though Brielle herself didn't. Someone truly stuck up wouldn't come back to speed friendshipping, after all.

Brielle sniffs and looks down. I hope I didn't embarrass her. She'd probably rather forget about those comments.

"That's really nice, Jack," she finally says. "But it's not just one troll. A lot of people agree."

"Here's the thing. They're totally wrong, but I can see how you might come off that way to people who don't know you. Your MyTube is all full of makeup tutorials, fashion stuff, and all that. Maybe you could lighten things up. Make a funny video every now and then."

She shakes her head and lets out a sharp *ha*. "I'm terrible at being funny. It would just be awkward if I tried."

Here's where I come in.

I shrug and look at my nails. "I mean, I could help you

if you want. We could do a video or two together. That way people can see you can have a sense of humor."

Brielle eyes me suspiciously. "Why would you want to help me? It's not like we're friends. No offense."

I grab the back of my neck. I didn't plan for a line of questioning. "I'm a really good person?" I squeak out.

She crosses her arms. "Tell me the real reason, or I don't need your help."

"Okay, okay. My parents grounded me from my phone. And MyTube. I miss it."

She nods slowly. "So, you're afraid if you stop posting, then people will forget about you."

"Forget about me?" I laugh uncomfortably. She stares at me like she's playing psychiatrist and looking deep into my soul, which I definitely didn't give her permission to do. "Nah. I just like making videos. So, what do you think? Can we help each other?"

She bites her lip. "I guess we can do one video, just to see how it goes. But not anything gross, like blowing milk out of our noses or anything like that."

"So you've seen my videos." The milk one was my first.

"Just a couple." She blinks. "But I've never seen that one. Not that I'm surprised it exists. So, what do you have in mind?"

The woman volunteer walks up to us and lingers. "Having fun?" she asks perkily, her bright white teeth shining between her brown lipstick. I nod, but Brielle turns pink and glares at the woman. The woman gets the hint and moves down the aisle. I've never seen Brielle act rude to an adult before. Wait . . . they're both blond and have light blue eyes.

"Is that your mom?"

Brielle shushes me angrily and then composes herself, tucking her hair behind her ear and straightening up in her chair. "It doesn't matter. We were talking about your video idea."

I want to ask why she's so embarrassed, but Busby could ring the bell any second and I'm running out of time. "There's this thing I've been wanting to try. We'd have to be somewhere where lots of people are walking around."

"Maybe the mall? What's the idea?"

"Yeah, the mall would work. When can you meet up?"

She pulls up her phone calendar. "I'm pretty busy this weekend, but I can probably do something tomorrow between twelve and one-thirty. Now, stop avoiding the question. What's the idea?"

"Switch!" says Mr. Busby.

"Ohh, too bad." I stand. "Guess I'll have keep you in suspense."

"Ugh, you're the worst."

"Meet me at the mall tomorrow. At noon in the food court, in front of Hot Dog on a Spork. I won't have my phone, so you can't text me if you're late."

"I'm never late."

Getting Brielle there is only half the challenge. Getting her to participate will be the other. Because if she thinks having her mom at speed friendshipping is embarrassing, then I'm not sure she'll be up for what I have planned.

Unless it turns out that what Mr. Busby said is true: "Sometimes people will surprise you."

Tasha

Tasha:

It's so awkward that Brielle and I haven't talked since we hung out last Saturday. I only came to speed friendshipping because I thought she wouldn't show up anyway. But when I walked into the drama room, the first thing I saw was Brielle sitting there, ankles crossed down at the side of her chair like how they teach princesses to sit in movies. I almost walked right back out the doors, but I knew that would look pretty strange. Instead I made sure to sit in her same row so we wouldn't be forced to talk. Plus, Mario was sitting in the opposite row, and I wanted to get paired with him. Can you blame me?

Mario has the cutest dimple on his chin and the kind of smile that makes you forget what you were saying midsentence. His hair looks permanently wind-blown, even when it's not windy. During our turn, he told me about his favorite sports, and I told him about my fashion designs. Talking to him is comfortable. It never feels like he's digging through his mind for something to say. I bet he's the kind of person I could even talk to about DeAndre and he wouldn't be weird about it.

Even talking to Jack was fun today. He taught me all about the "art of T-rexing." I'm not planning on busting out roaring anytime soon, but it was amusing nonetheless. Brielle and I, however, didn't exchange any words besides "hi." Her mom ended up talking to me more than she did. Not that I'm surprised.

Here's the backstory. Last Saturday, Brielle texted me saying she and her friend Devyn were going to make cookies if I wanted to join. At first, I was hesitant. I knew she felt obligated to invite me, and I doubted we'd have anything in common. I mean, I wear bright patterns and unexpected combinations, while she dresses like she's about to hit up a tea party. But I really wanted cookies. And I *needed* to get out of my house. Mom and I pulled the tile out that morning, and everything was covered in a layer of fine dust. I feel like I'm going to get a lung disease from breathing so much of it in.

Brielle lives in exactly the kind of house you would've guessed. First you walk through an iron gate, and then through double front doors with a large knocker. Inside it's decorated like all the home accounts on MyTube: potted plants on floating shelves, walls covered with giant mirrors, and photos of her smiling on the beach with her parents.

Devyn bailed, so it ended up being just Brielle and me. She took charge of the cookie making, and I mostly measured the ingredients. It was going okay, even though we were mostly talking about the things on her to-do list (and I knew I was one of those things). To be fair, when I showed her my fashion account, she loved it, which was flattering. I almost asked if she'd give my account a shout-out, but I didn't want to push it. She has tons of followers, so it'd be nice to get some of them to check me out. Most of my followers only follow me because they are also fashion accounts and they want a follow back. It's faker than middle school.

After we put the cookies into the oven, Brielle's mom came in with her hair in curlers and started asking me about where I lived and what I like to do. Then she started going over student council campaign strategies with Brielle. She wants her to pass out doughnut holes with a note attached on a toothpick saying, "DO-NUT think twice, vote for Brielle!" Brielle apologized afterward for her mom butting in, but I didn't mind. She's lucky her mom cares enough to ask her about her life. It used to be like that with my mom. Ever since DeAndre died, she only talks to me about renovations. We can't all be perfect families.

The cookies turned out amazing, partially because we were using these large, chunky Ghirardelli chocolate chips. We separated some cookies out for the girls in Brielle's church group, and Brielle let me take the rest since she's on a sugar-free diet with her mom. Why people would put themselves through that kind of torture is beyond me.

Anyway, hanging out was obviously a one-time thing. At least I got cookies out of it.

All that baking gave me an idea. Mom will probably hate it, but I'm going to bring it up to her tonight.

DeAndre's birthday is next Wednesday, and I want to do something special for him. I also want an excuse to invite Dad over. He lives an hour and a half away, and I haven't seen him in almost two months. He and Mom are going through a divorce. That's right. My brother died *and* my parents are splitting up. Sometimes I feel like a walking Lifetime movie.

The counselor Mom made me talk to after we moved here told me that couples are more likely to split up after the death of a child. Isn't that messed up? You'd think death would bring people together, and help them realize how much they love each other. For some families, it does. But for us, DeAndre's death turned my parents into zombies who *stopped* loving each other.

Real life is so upside down sometimes.

The thing that makes me the angriest—like, want-

to-punch-a-hole-in-our-newly-textured-walls angry—
is that this is the exact opposite of what DeAndre
would have wanted.

People sometimes say he's watching over us. I'm
not sure about that, because I bet that in heaven, they
have more interesting things to do than pay attention
to boring old earth. But what if he does take a peek
every now and then? How would he feel knowing his
death drove my parents apart?

Right before the funeral, I was hiding under my
bedcovers. I didn't want to face all those people telling me they were sorry, when they could never understand. Mom came into my room and gave me a hug
and a kiss on the head. She told me the best way to
honor DeAndre was to keep our chins up and live our
lives to the fullest. She said that hard things can make
us stronger or weaker. We can choose to be either a
potato or an egg: both get put in boiling water, but the
egg gets hard and the potato gets soft. I guess you're
supposed to be the egg.

I felt like the potato. And since my parents gave up
on their marriage, they ended up being potatoes too.
If only Mom could've taken her own advice.

That's why I want DeAndre to be able to see some
good things, on the chance he does look down. I want
him to see how he influenced me to become a fashion

designer. I want him to see us all together on his birthday, eating a cake I baked in his honor.

His favorite was German chocolate. Maybe I could even throw in the good kind of chocolate chips that Brielle had at her house.

Mario:

So I guess Jack hates me now. I should've seen it coming. I got his phone taken away, and that's *the* most important thing in the world to him. It's not even my fault. I just happen to have a mother who thinks MyTube is the root of all evil. She freaked out when she saw the video her nosy friend sent her. "Why would you want a bunch of strangers watching you throw food at each other?" Mom said at dinner. "I don't get it." She'll never get it. She doesn't understand what's funny.

I was hoping I'd see Jack at speed friendshipping and things would feel normal again, but instead, he's giving me the silent treatment. He didn't so much as look in my direction during the rounds. When it was over, I wanted to ask him about his Pokémon tryouts, but before I could reach him, he took a handful of Jolly Ranchers and left. That's not even good candy.

It's pretty obvious what's going on. Jack was using me because he thought I'd be his talent show partner and video sidekick. Now that I can't, he's through with me. It stinks because I had a lot of fun at his house, but he's the type of guy who can get any friend he wants, so why would he stick with someone who can't do the stuff he likes?

What's ironic is that my plan to get Perry a new friend is working, so now I'm double friendless. Perry met Phineas at speed friendshipping last week, and they were destined to be friends from the start. They're both super into this anime show I tried watching once and couldn't get into, and they follow all the same MyTubers and watch them play video games. I'll never understand what's fun about watching other people game. Perry says it's like watching sports, only the sport is gaming. It makes sense in theory, but still— boring!

Maybe I'm the boring one. Maybe I'm like my mom, and I just don't get it. I wish I could find someone who likes the stuff I do, but there's no hacky sack club at school, and I didn't think I'd have time to join soccer league this year.

Luckily, Phineas has a different lunch period, or he'd be sitting with us every day geeking out over fandom stuff. He and Perry are always texting. Apparently there's this cartoon where a guy named Phineas has a pet platypus named Perry, so they send lots of platypus memes back and forth and make platypus calls to each other. Who knew platypuses made noises? It's a soft, squeaky purr, like a cat that swallowed a rubber mouse.

If Mom would just let me have a phone, things would be different. Jack and I would be friends and make tons of videos. People around school would know who I am, the way they know him. I could text without my mom seeing everything people say to me.

Could I ever convince Mom that I'm responsible enough for a phone? I get A's and B's, and I never get detention. She thinks the internet's full of creepers, but I could research how to spot red flags. She thinks phones are addicting, but I could promise to only use my phone for a couple of hours a day. If I turn this into a reasonable enough argument, maybe, just maybe, she'd hear me out.

When I was eight, I wanted a dog more than anything in the world, and (as usual) Mom said no. I begged and begged, but she wouldn't budge. My tío Antonio was on my side. He always is. He helped me put together a slideshow about the benefits of having a dog and the responsibilities I would accept if I got one. Mom was so impressed that she let me get a goldfish. Not a dog, but it was better than nothing. Mr. Bubbles and I enjoyed a blissful five months together until he ran away one day to join the circus.

Wait . . .

Note to self: ask Mom what really happened to Mr. Bubbles.

Anyway, the point is that maybe the same strategy would work this time. Now that I'm older, I could make the bullet points myself and cite websites and stuff like we're learning to do in English.

I want a phone even more than I wanted a dog.

Brielle:

I hope Tasha and Jack are the only ones who realized my mom was at speed friendshipping. She's soooo beyond embarrassing. She always shows up to my dance classes, she's friends with all my teachers, and she likes every single one of my MyTube videos. At least I got her to stop commenting. ("My daughter is a queen!" *Ughhhh.*)

Brielle

Now I'm starting to worry she's jeopardizing my

chances at winning the student council election by making me look like I don't want to play fair. Today she was trying to convince Mr. Busby (quite loudly, might I add) to abolish the rule where student council candidates can't bring in treats as part of their campaign.

She nudged his arm. "The school needs to loosen up! Let the kids have some fun."

He smiled politely. "You'll have to take that issue up with the principal."

She will, Mr. Busby. She will.

Mom's . . . *involvement* got extra bad at the beginning of this school year, right after Dad left. They weren't always fighting anymore, so Mom had all this extra time and energy to butt into every aspect of my life. ("It's just you and me now. We get to have girl time!") Mom said Dad wouldn't be gone forever, that they only needed a break. It ended up being eight and a half weeks.

During those weeks, Mom didn't tell anyone what was going on. When neighbors or people at church asked about Dad, she said he was on a work trip. "Some truths are too hard to explain," she told me. I think she was just embarrassed. So was I.

That's when Mom joined the parent-teacher committee, which is also where she heard about speed friendshipping. ("That sounds so adorable! I *have* to come watch.") I came today to keep tabs on her. I needed to make sure she wasn't chatting too much with my classmates or trying to campaign on my behalf. I tried to get Devyn to come too so at least I'd have a friend here, but she thought it sounded "super dumb."

Devyn's been getting on my nerves lately. Last Saturday, she ditched out on making cookies with me and Tasha, and I found out later she went to Celine's house instead. Why wouldn't they invite me? Am I not fun enough?

I was dreading being left alone with Tasha. I barely knew her, so I thought having another person around would minimize the awkwardness potential. It ended up being chill, though. We just baked and talked about school and random stuff. She's kind of quiet, so it's hard to gauge if she had fun too. Either way, I invited her over first, so now it's her turn to invite me. And she probably won't. She hasn't said anything to me since Saturday, so I don't think she's interested in being friends. She probably has enough friends already. The group she sits with at lunch seems pretty tight.

That's fine, though, because I don't have time to hang out anyway. I'm pushing the limit as it is by making this video with Jack. But his videos are popular, and he has lots of followers, so his stamp of approval could help me beat Zane—aka the guy everyone thinks is cool but is actually a huge jerk. I never liked him ever since he shot me in the back of the head with a water gun at his pool party—and I had just gotten my first highlights! Losing to him would be worse than ripping off a hangnail.

Hopefully whatever Jack has planned can be squeezed into the two-hour window between the church service project and my dance recital.

13

Going Old-School

It's 12:01 and I'm in front of Hot Dog on a Spork, just like I said I'd be. Brielle is officially late. She's probably standing me up. Did I really think *she* would want in on one of my videos? The smiling hot dog on the neon sign seems to be mocking me. I glare back at it.

"Hey, Jack. Sorry I'm late."

I whirl around so fast, I almost hit Brielle with my backpack. Her vanilla perfume mixed with the scent of corn dog smells surprisingly tasty. I wonder if corn dogs dipped in ice cream would taste as good as fries dipped in milkshake.

I shrug like I wasn't even worried. "You're literally one minute late. You're fine."

"So, what's this brilliant idea? I only have an hour. My dance recital is tonight, and my mom's taking me to get my hair done."

"Let's sit." I lead her to one of the food court tables. It's gunky and spotted with puddles of what I really hope is lemonade.

I sit and scoot my chair back from the nasty table. "My dad was telling me about this game he used to play as a kid. It's called the clothespin challenge."

"What do you do? Clip them onto your nose or something?"

"Even better. Clip them onto other people."

She lifts an eyebrow. "What?"

I pull a bag of clothespins from my backpack. "Other, unsuspecting people. Basically, we both get five clothespins. We time how long it takes to clip them on five different people. Whoever does it the fastest wins."

Brielle taps her fingernails on the table, but they don't clack because she's chewed them down to the nub. "Are you serious?"

"Dead. Oh, and if you get caught, you're disqualified."

She stands. "Okay, this was a bad idea. You can't just clip clothespins on people, Jack. That's rude and embarrassing. I should leave." She grabs her purse. "I have so much to do today."

"That's fine," I say casually. "But this would be the perfect way to prove you're not uptight. Imagine everyone seeing you take this risk. Living on the edge. You call it embarrassing. I call it instant respect."

"Ugh." She hesitates and then slowly sits back down. "I'll do one clothespin. Just one. But you're going first."

"My pleasure. Now, record me so I can explain the rules."

"Fine." She points her phone at me. "Go."

"*Heyooooo.* Brielle and Jack here—collab edition! We're just chillin' at the mall, and we have this awesome thing we're gonna do. It's called the"—I sing the words—"*clothespin challenge.* Have you heard of the clothespin challenge, Brielle?"

"Yeah, you just told me about it."

"Pause!"

She puts down her phone. "What?"

"You've gotta play along. Just say no so I can explain it."

"Whatever."

We repeat the intro, and this time she says, "Why, no, Jack. Whatever is the clothespin challenge?" It's a little snarky, but I explain the rules anyway.

I clip a clothespin to my nose so my voice sounds nasally. "I'm going first. Ready to time me, Bri Bri?"

"Don't call me that, and yes."

I unclip the clothespin and slip it into my back pocket. I motion for Brielle to follow me as I wander out of the food court into high traffic. Who should be my first victim?

The big guy with the muscle shirt? Don't wanna mess with him.

The old lady with the walking stick? Nah, she could use that thing as a weapon.

The mom with the double stroller? Yes. She's distracted trying to get one kid's shoe back on his foot.

I walk up next to the mom and pretend to admire the display window—which is probably weird because there are little-girl mannequins wearing butterfly skirts, but oh well. I sneakily pull a clothespin from my pocket and clip it onto the bottom of her skirt while she's scolding the other toddler for squeezing milk out of his sippy cup. Then I briskly walk away. Across the crowd, Brielle covers her mouth and her eyes crinkle. Hopefully she got a clear shot.

I've got to be faster. A little kid is gawking over the cupcake tower in the display window of Sweets 'n' Stuff. I tiptoe behind him and clip a clothespin on the side pocket of his pants. He swivels his head toward me but doesn't say anything, so it totally doesn't count as getting caught.

Next I enter the pet store and clothespin an employee, as well as a middle-aged man tapping on the mouse-cage glass. Brielle follows close behind, catching everything as sneakily as one can while holding a phone in front of their face.

One clothespin left. I exit the pet shop and spot a teenage girl sitting on a bench next to a plant. She's texting and totally oblivious to her surroundings. Perfect.

As I head toward the texter, I turn around to make sure Brielle's in a good recording position. I take a step backward and my shoulder bumps into the rubber plant next to the bench, causing it to topple over. I grab on to one of the rubbery leaves and pull it back up. Brielle's burst of laughter echoes out across the walkway. So much for being stealthy.

Amazingly, my target is still texting. She hasn't moved a muscle, except for the thumb ones.

I clip the clothespin onto the collar of her jacket and run back to Brielle.

"Final time: six minutes and thirty-two seconds," she says.

"Not bad!" I high-five her with both hands.

"I gotta give it to you, Jack. You have no shame."

"One of my only good qualities."

She laughs. "My turn, I guess. You really think I can do this?" Her breathing gets faster and she starts bouncing around like she maybe has to pee.

"Of course you can. You're way less suspicious-looking than I am. If I didn't get caught, you definitely won't."

"Good point." She breathes in deeply and squeezes her hands together. "I'm just doing one, though. That's all I have to do to look fun, right?"

"One is better than nothing, but I'd automatically win."

Brielle closes her eyes. "I can do this, I can do this," she whispers to herself. I try not to snort. She hands me her phone. "Tell me when to go."

I press the Record button. "Go! You got this, Bri Bri." She's so focused on her breathing that she doesn't even tell me to not call her that again.

"I'm going for that guy." She jabs her thumb at a middle-aged dude sitting in a massage recliner in the middle of the walkway. His eyes are closed and he's maybe even asleep. Great target. The texting girl has left the bench, so I stand next to it and record from behind the plant.

Brielle walks to the recliner with jerky motions—fast, and then slow, and then fast, and then slow. She peeks over her shoulder and quickly clips the clothespin to the man's sleeve. He snores loudly, causing her to jump, but he stays asleep.

She jogs back to me and squeals. "I did it! I really did it! He didn't even see me!"

"Well, he had his eyes closed, so yeah, I'd be impressed if he did see you."

She bounces on the balls of her feet. "Wasn't that awesome? What'll he do when he wakes up and sees it? Oh my gosh, he's going to be so confused! Oh my gosh, should I go take it off?"

"I think he'll be fine. People can always use an extra clothespin." I stop recording. "Well, you accomplished your goal. You can forfeit now if you'd like."

"No way! I'm going to crush you. How long were you recording?"

I check. "Twenty-seven seconds."

"And your time was six thirty-two. I have four clothespins left, and six minutes to beat you. Easy!" She darts into Bath & Body Works and I follow. So the girl's got a competitive side. Didn't see that coming.

Brielle sneaks up behind a lady sniffing a candle and snips the second clothespin onto the rim of her sun hat. Brilliant. Then she follows a small family out of the store and gets the shirt of one of the little kids, who's probably about five years old. And she said *I* had no shame!

Next she gets a teenage guy standing in line for Cinnabon by clipping a clothespin onto the rim of his backward-turned baseball cap. Brielle is truly a natural. I should've thought to target more people with hats. If I ever do this again, that'll be my strategy.

"One more!" she mouths.

Ten feet in front of us, an elderly woman with a sheer blue scarf spritzes perfume samples at a kiosk. It would be so easy to clip a clothespin onto that scarf.

Brielle and I lock eyes as if reading each other's minds.

She walks swiftly to the kiosk and lifts the woman's scarf with her left hand while holding the clothespin with her right hand. The woman steps forward just at the moment Brielle's clipping on the clothespin, and the scarf tugs around her neck.

The lady's head jerks toward Brielle. "What in tarnation?" she croaks. She looks at the kiosk worker. "This young lady is trying to steal my scarf! Right off my neck!"

Brielle stands frozen. "I . . . I . . ."

I feel bad for laughing, but how could I not? "Run!" I shout. This'll make for prime entertainment.

Brielle looks at me, and then at the lady. Then back at me, and back at the lady. Then she sprints off.

"Get her!" the lady orders the kiosk worker. He blinks, frozen with confusion. "I said get her!" she insists more loudly, and he abandons his perfume stand to chase us.

We turn the corner and I point the camera at myself midrun. "They're . . . they're on our tail!" I say through exaggerated panting.

I focus the camera on Brielle. "Twelve years old and already a felon. How do you think you'll handle jail?"

"Oh, shut up! Let's hide in here." She turns sharply into Build-A-Bear Workshop and ducks behind one of the giant teddy bears on display. I crouch beside her.

I record the fuzzy blue bear and whisper. "This is the great Mr. Cuddles. They say his protective charm will hide us from outside forces." Brielle shushes me.

The kiosk worker jogs past the Build-A-Bear Workshop entrance, and we both release our breaths.

"That was close," Brielle says. "Seriously close. I mean, I wonder what he would have . . . wait. Why are you smiling like that?"

"Because you got caught. Therefore you are disqualified. Therefore . . . I win!"

I do my signature happy dance where I swing my elbows and bop my head from left to right: "Uh-huh. Oh, yeah. Uh-huh. Oh, yeah."

"That's so unfair!" She punches my arm. "I was so much faster!"

"Rules are rules." I point the camera at myself and say, "There you have it, folks. Jack Reynolds is the clothespin champion! Gotta run!"

An employee leans over us and squints. "Is everything all right? Did you drop something down there?"

"Oh. Yeah," says Brielle, sweeping her hand across the wood floor. "My earring. I've got it."

We stand, and Brielle checks her phone for the time. "Well, I should get out of here before the kiosk man comes back this way. My mom'll be picking me up soon in front of Nordstrom anyway."

"Okay," I say. I almost offer to walk her to Nordstrom, but I figure she's probably had enough of me for one day. "Send me that footage and I'll edit it on my laptop. I'll send it back by tonight for you to upload."

"Will do."

I grab a bear and squeeze its plushy foot. "Good luck at your recital tonight."

"Thanks." She pauses in the entryway of the store. "I actually had a lot of fun. I think this video will be a good one."

"Me too. People are gonna love seeing this side of you."

I sure did.

14

A New Plan

I pass by Brielle's desk before first period on Monday. This weekend has been a weird form of torture. I know Brielle uploaded our video Saturday night, but I haven't been able to see any of the reactions. It feels like I'm locked out of a house with a big party going on inside. On Sunday, I snuck Jacob's phone off his nightstand while he was napping so I could check MyTube, but I couldn't get past his fingerprint password lock. He woke up right as I was pressing his thumb to the keypad. Now I have to do his laundry for two weeks or he'll tell Mom.

I kneel next to Brielle's desk. "How's our felon doing this morning?"

"Ha ha, very funny." She lowers her voice. "My mom wasn't thrilled about our video. Next time, we have to do something that's 'less invasive of people's personal space.'"

"So, what you're saying is that there will be a next time."

"If we can make another video that catches on like this one, then sure. I mean, look at all these shares." She checks that Ms. Campbell isn't watching, and then slides her phone from her purse into the shadow under her desk. Little Brielle, breaking rules left and right.

I look at her screen and my jaw drops. "Three thousand views and four hundred and eight shares? How?"

She slips her phone back into her pocket. "Right? I had no idea it would blow up like this!"

I wonder if it would've gotten as many shares if I had posted it on my account instead of hers. It was my idea, after all. "You tagged me, right?"

"Yeah."

"Good."

Brielle's friend Devyn walks up to us and brushes her fingers through Brielle's hair. "I can't believe you didn't invite me to the mall with you guys. You have to invite me to your next video."

Brielle winces. Either she doesn't like other people playing with her hair, or she doesn't like the idea of Devyn joining in.

The girl in front of us turns around. "That video was hilarious. Especially when that old lady thought you were stealing her scarf." She and Brielle crack up.

I almost want to point out that the whole thing was my idea, but I'll let Brielle have her moment. She looks like she's enjoying it.

Zane calls from two rows over, "Brielle, that was probably the worst thing you've ever done in your life, huh?" He makes a high-pitched voice. *"Oooh, I put a clothespin on someone. I'm soooo bad."*

"Leave her alone," I say.

"I'm joking," he says. "Chill out, *coolio.*"

I clench my teeth. How dare he use our old greeting ironically just to spite me.

Brielle smiles a little, but her eyes look sad. "The bell's about to ring. You'd better get to your seat."

I almost say, *Yes, Mother,* but it feels like the wrong time to say something like that.

At lunch, I sit with my milk-spitter crew again, but I stop by Brielle's table during the last ten minutes for a view count update. Our shares are up past five hundred. It's so unfair that I couldn't post this on my own account. I don't know if I'll ever forgive Mom and Dad. Brielle lets me read through some comments, and there's a wide variety: compliments ("Brielle, you always look sooo cute"), awkwardness ("Wait, are you guys dating?"), suggestions ("You shoulda clipped it on the sleeping guy's nose!"), and, as always, randomness ("I ate a pickle for lunch, just thought you should know"). There are a couple of mean comments here or there, but nothing that I think would seriously hurt Brielle's feelings. Hopefully it stays that way.

Mario's table is next to Brielle's, so when I look up from the phone, we make eye contact. He waves, and I wave back. I'm glad that even though we're not friends anymore, it looks like we're on good terms. Maybe I'll even sit with him and Perry occasionally, as a backup to my backup crew. I'll just have to make sure to not do anything that gets him in trouble again.

Wednesday marks one week of being without my phone, and it feels like a reasonable time to ask for it back. I've been a straight-up angel child. I've done all my chores without complaining. I offered to rub Dad's smelly feet. I even spent two hours yesterday planting thorny plants around the trash bins. They're supposed to deter the raccoons, who, it turns out, were not afraid of the blinking lights.

I plan to bring it up at dinner. Josh is eating over at a friend's house (lucky duck), so it's just Jacob, my parents, and me. Mom calls everyone into the kitchen to dish up. We scoop the spaghetti out of the pot on the counter and pile it onto our plates. I give myself extra salad, hoping Mom notices, and sit at the table.

"I got an email from your teacher, Jack," Mom says, sitting down next to me. My fork freezes on its way to my mouth. This can't be good. I review the day's events. My social studies teacher got mad at me for eating a PB and J during a quiz, and my science teacher chewed me out for rubber-banding my ears together. But I get along with both of them. Would they really rat me out like that?

"Which teacher?" I ask.

"Your math teacher."

Then it hits. The F.

Yesterday Ms. Snyder passed back our tests. She always puts them on our desks facedown, but people still try to glance at other people's scores. I carefully raised the corner of my test just until I saw the grade in red ink, and then quickly stuffed it into my binder. It was a 47 percent. That's bad, even for me. I probably should have studied this weekend instead of editing the clothespin video.

Getting a bad grade, no matter how used to it you are, always makes you feel like someone clipped a string you didn't realize was holding you up. What's worse is hearing how everyone else did better than you. "Wow, you got a hundred!" the kid behind Tasha said yesterday when she lifted her test. Of course she did. Tasha shrugged ever so slightly, looking embarrassed but proud at the same time.

"What did you get?" people started whispering to each other. "What about you?" Why can't everyone mind their own business? I knew I was gonna get asked eventually, so I decided to own up to it. "An F?" I slammed my fist on my desk. "This is a disgrace! I studied for a solid three minutes! Ms. Snyder, I'd like to speak to your superior!"

Everyone laughed and started talking about how long *they* studied.

"Three minutes? I spent an hour!"

"I spent two!"

In the end, I looked like I was lazy. Not just dumb.

Mom puts her fork down. "She says you're in danger of failing her class."

"It depends on your definition of failing."

"The definition of failing is getting an F," Dad says.

I purse my lips. "I think I have, like, a sixty-three-point-something? That's not so close to an F, right?"

Jacob snorts. "Yeah, not close at all." I glare at him. Did Mom *really* have to bring this up in front of Jacob? And did Ms. Snyder *really* have to let Mom know? As surprising as it is, I've rarely had teachers email home about bad stuff I've done. Even Ms. Campbell never emailed Mom about the marshmallow darts. Sure, my teachers can get annoyed with me, but I try to stay on most of their good sides. We have inside jokes and all that. I'm a straight-C student who dips only briefly into the D range every now and then.

Ms. Snyder is probably the teacher who likes me the least. She must have never gotten over that time I told everyone to sniff when she faced the whiteboard.

"It'll be fine." I swallow a bite of salad and keep my voice calm. "I forgot to study for a test that turned out to be a bigger part of our grade than I thought. I'll do better on the next one."

Dad shakes his head. "This wasn't because of one test, Jack. This is indicative of a lack of effort throughout the entire semester."

So much for my plan to ask for my phone back. I can already feel the punishment coming. What else can Mom and Dad take from me? Maybe they'll give me an early bedtime. Or not let me watch movies.

I wonder if they'd let me choose my own punishment. The thorny plants I planted by the trash bins haven't been working, so I could offer to keep watch at night and be the official raccoon chaser. I could set up all these elaborate booby traps. That would make a hilarious video.

If I had a phone, that is.

Mom rests her hand on Dad's forearm. "Your father and I have been talking. You've gone a week without your phone, and we've been impressed by your behavior so far. We were going to give your phone back this weekend, but now we'll have to wait until you get your math grade up."

I try not to look excited, because I know they're hoping this is bad news for me. Actually, I'm relieved. My phone is within reach. There's finally a light at the end of this dark, lonely tunnel. "What grade do I need?"

"If you can get your grade up to a C, you can have your phone back," Mom says. "With limits, that is."

"What kind of limits?"

Mom scoots her chair back and walks to the hutch. She opens the door and pulls out a wicker basket. "Starting tomorrow, we'll all be turning our phones in to this basket before dinner, and we won't get them back until the next morning."

"What?" says Jacob. "I use my phone as an alarm. How will I wake up?"

Dad smirks. "You'll have to get an alarm clock. So old-school."

"Why am I getting punished because of something Jack did?" He moans.

"It's not a punishment," Mom says. "Screen time at night is terrible for your sleeping patterns. My friend sent me an article about it."

I bet that was Mario's mom. It sounds *so* like her.

"I think this is a great idea," I say, hoping for once to look like the good child in comparison to Jacob. Mom smiles. She returns to the table and nudges Dad. "See? That went over better than we thought."

Just a week ago, I would have hated the basket idea, but now it doesn't sound so bad. At least I'll get my phone for most of the day. It's better than nothing.

We have our final exam coming up in math next week. I wonder if acing it could get my overall grade up to 70 percent.

I've never been so motivated to study in my entire life. And I know just the person who can help me.

15

Grandpa Jack

I never thought this day would come. I thought that first pigs would fly, aliens would land, Brielle would burp the alphabet. But it's time I admitted the cold, hard truth: I need a tutor.

Mom has suggested I get tutored a billion times, and I've always refused. Who wants to do extra schoolwork when they don't have to? Last semester, my school started a peer-tutor program where they paired smart kids with "struggling students" for homework help. I snuck into Mom's email and deleted the message the school sent out because I knew she'd be all over it. How embarrassing would it be to be one of the "dumb kids" that needs help from a "peer."

Yet here I am, at speed friendshipping round three,

seeking out my own tutor. A cruel twist of fate. But desperate times call for desperate measures.

The first person I notice when I walk into the drama room is Mr. Busby. He's wearing a neon-green suit jacket that could blind you if you stare at it too long, kind of like looking into the sun. It reminds me of a lime Popsicle. Speaking of which, what treats do they have today?

Ah, Kevin's chocolate chip cookies. An upgrade from Jolly Ranchers, for sure. They sit waiting for us on the table by the old piano. Most of the cookie plates are covered in foil, but one plate has the foil bent back. Someone must have snuck a cookie early.

The next person I notice is Tasha, who I came here for. My shoulders relax now that I know she's here.

Tasha's always getting the highest grades in our math class. If I can get her to help me ace my next test, my phone will be back in my rightful hands within the week.

Maybe. I'm not actually sure what percentage of our grade this test will be. I wonder if Ms. Snyder would jack up the amount of points it's worth. I have a feeling my marshmallow-bribing trick wouldn't work on her, though.

I meant to talk to Tasha yesterday, but she sits by the door in math and always leaves before me. I take the seat opposite her and look around. Perry's here, but not Mario. Brielle's gone too. Earlier she told me she had to record her student council speech after school.

I'd been considering asking Brielle to tutor me instead of Tasha since I know her better, but I'd rather not add to her stress since she's so busy. Still, she wants to make another video on Saturday. I think she expects me to come up with the idea, but so far, I've got nothing. It's hard to be creative when I know I won't get the credit. It stinks that we can only post on her page, since Mom is snooping around mine.

Mr. Busby stands up front and flaps out the sides of his suit jacket like he's going to fly away. "I can't believe not one person has asked me about my fantastic outfit!"

Now it makes sense. The jacket is some sort of lesson, which means it's okay to make fun of it. "Fine, you asked for it," I say. "Why are you dressed like a highlighter?"

Mr. Busby grins. "Can anyone think of a more tactful way to ask me about my jacket?"

Dead silence. There's no way to be tactful about that thing.

He paces the room. "Okay, what about, 'What a unique jacket! Is green your favorite color?' or, 'Have you considered modeling?'"

"I think it's bold," Tasha says. "I'd ask where you got it from."

"That's a wonderful question! I got this jacket at a thrift store in my hometown, Possum Grape, Arkansas."

"Possum Grape?" I ask. "Is that for real?"

"It is." He sweeps his arm. "And, see? Now a conversation

has started. I can tell you about my hometown and how it got its name. I can tell you about my love of thrift-store shopping, and the creative ways I try to save money. Asking people about what they're wearing is an easy and natural way to strike up a conversation. So today, find an object to ask your partner about. Their jewelry, a hairstyle, a piece of clothing. Even a sticker on a binder, or a pin on a backpack. There are a lot of us today, so we'll just try to get through as many rounds as possible. And remember . . ."

He points at us because by now we should know what he's gonna say:

"There's nothing more interesting than people," half of us mumble.

Mr. Busby dings the bell, and I look at Tasha. I want to ask about tutoring right away, but she seems like a follow-the-rules-of-the-game type of person. I'm gonna have to slide into it naturally.

"So, your socks," Tasha says without hesitation.

I stick my leg out. "You mean these bad boys?" My jeans are rolled up to more fully display Josh's Cheez-Its socks. I gave him the idea to buy them, so I figured it was okay to secretly borrow them.

She snorts. "Who even thinks up this stuff?"

"Geniuses, obviously."

"Why do you always wear funny socks?"

I shrug. "I have since fourth grade." I still remember my

first pair: black with red chile peppers. I begged my mom to buy them.

Tasha tilts her head. "What made you start?"

It's not a particularly good memory. I've never talked about it to anyone. But Tasha's looking at me with wide-open eyes like she's really interested.

I sigh. "I wore these ugly white socks to school one day, and a kid in my class made fun of them. He said they were grandpa socks because they went halfway up my calves. They were hand-me-downs from my older brother."

She frowns. "Kids can be jerks."

"He was just kidding, but yeah."

"You were embarrassed, then?"

"I guess so." I kick my toe on the ground. "It's funny because when you're a little kid, you don't really think about your clothes. You just wear whatever dorky thing your mom puts you in. And then one day, you realize people are paying attention."

"I get what you mean. So, what did you say to him?"

"I don't remember, but I started talking in a grandpa voice. I picked up a stick and pretended it was my cane. For the rest of the day, people called me Grandpa Jack."

"I guess that's a good way to deal with it."

"Yeah, but the teacher got mad at me and made me stop using the grandpa voice. Which was good, because it was making my throat hurt."

She shakes her head and smiles. "You haven't changed much, have you?"

The bell dings. Was that two minutes already? "Mr. Busby," I call out. "You didn't tell us when time was half up."

"Ah, sorry." He presses his fist to his forehead. "Guess I forgot."

I stay seated as the guy next to us hovers by my chair. "But I didn't get to ask Tasha about anything she was wearing."

I also didn't get to ask her about tutoring, which was my whole point of coming here.

Mr. Busby winks. "Good thing you can always talk after the rounds are over."

"Come on. Can we please have one more round together?" I point to the guy hovering by me. "He can skip over us. It wouldn't mess anything up."

Mr. Busby looks like he's considering it, so I hammer in the final nail. "We're having a really rich conversation. I feel like we're making a friendship connection."

"Fine. Just this once." He motions for the kid to skip over us. Score!

Tasha pulls a face. "A *friendship connection*?"

Looking back on it, that was pretty embarrassing. "I wanted to ask you a favor," I admit.

Tasha folds her arms. "So *that's* what this is about. What's the favor?"

I lean in and lower my voice. "What would you think about tutoring me a couple of times before the math final next Wednesday? I need to get my grade up to a C."

She lifts an eyebrow. "Are you grounded or something?"

"Worse. My parents took my phone away. For practically no reason, too. It was totally unfair."

"I should've known," she says, smirking. "You haven't checked your phone this entire conversation."

"Ooh, burn. Fair enough."

Tasha unfolds her arms. "I guess I can try to help, but I can't guarantee you'll do well. I've never tutored before."

"No worries," I say before she changes her mind. "Could you do tomorrow?"

"Sure. But it'd have to be before noon."

"How about ten?"

"That works."

I dig through my backpack for a pen and paper. "Can you write your address down?" It'd be easier for her to text it to me, but that's obviously not an option.

She stares at the pen and winces. "Can we do it at your house instead?"

I'd rather not have a girl over. My brothers would tease

me and say she was my girlfriend. I know because Josh and I did that to Jacob once. He's probably eager to repay the favor.

"We have a raccoon infestation. I can't risk you getting rabies."

"Okay . . . What about the library?"

I'd also rather not be seen studying in public. "Why not your house?"

Tasha shuffles her feet. "My house is kind of a disaster. We're . . . renovating."

"Oh, like on *Home Flipperz*? I love that show!"

Tasha rolls her eyes. "No, it's the worst! It's all lies. Renovating is dusty, and smelly, and . . . did I mention dusty? There's enough dust to make a sandcastle!"

"Ha! Now I double want to come over."

"Fine. But don't say I didn't warn you about my house. I expect payment in the form of cherry Slurpees."

"Done."

"One minute left!" Mr. Busby yells as Tasha's writing down her address. I guess there's time to talk about something she's wearing. I'm a little scared of the story behind the hat, but I've been curious about it for a while.

"So, your hats," I say, not knowing how to phrase a specific question. She asked about my socks the same way.

She tugs the side of her hat over her ear. "Yeah, they're . . . a big part of me, I guess. I crochet them myself."

"That's cool. Where'd you learn how?"

"Well." She takes a deep breath. "My grandma taught me. I first started making them for my brother when he lost his hair. He had cancer. He died last year."

"Oh man. I'm so sorry."

It gets quiet, like we're giving him a moment of silence. Her eyes cloud over with a sad, empty look, which makes me feel heavy inside. I never know what to say when people mention death. I don't want to press it if it's too hard to talk about. But I also want to show her I care.

"What was he like?" I finally ask.

She looks down and smiles a little. "Smart. Funny. He drove me to school every day and would blast the radio and sing really loud. I pretended I hated it, but it was actually fun."

Ding!

"He sounds like a really cool guy." I stand to rotate. "Thanks again for agreeing to tutor me."

"Well, we can't have you without your phone." She smiles mischievously. "You might actually learn something in class."

Tasha

Tasha:

I never thought the first person I'd talk to about DeAndre· at this school would be Jack Reynolds. I thought it'd be the girls I sit by at lunch, but they still don't even know I design clothes, much less anything about my family. It's probably better that I'm not close with them. It would make things harder when we move this summer.

Three other people asked about my hat today, but all those conversations went in different directions. Mei-ling went on to ask about my grandma; Michael asked if I also made scarves; and Axel asked if I could crochet him a hat with skulls and crossbones on it. I said sure, if he coughed up ten bucks. He said he'd get back to me.

Jack's the only one I told about DeAndre's cancer. I'm not sure why I told him the full truth. Maybe because he told me the story behind his socks, which felt pretty personal. I was surprised that he got embarrassed when someone made fun of him. I always assumed he didn't care what anyone thought.

I hope Mom doesn't make a big deal about Jack coming over tomorrow. She's always telling me I need to do stuff with people, so she'll probably be all excited that he's at our house, even though we're not really friends. She'd better not invite him to stay for dinner or say how grateful she is I have someone over or anything embarrassing like that.

I also hope Jack isn't shocked by the mess. I'll make sure we at least have the entryway vacuumed. Good thing he doesn't have his phone, so he can't make a video about it.

According to Mom's renovation chart, we'll finish this flip in three weeks, right around the last day of school. Mom says if we make a good profit, it might just take one more flip, and then we'll have enough money to keep a permanent home while flipping an extra. I wonder if our permanent home could be closer to where Dad's staying.

Last Friday while we were grouting the new tile, I told Mom about my idea to celebrate DeAndre's birthday. At first, she got real quiet, and all I could hear was the clink of her metal scraper against the floor. I was sure she was going to say no.

"That sounds wonderful, honey," she finally said. She smiled, but it was the fake kind that didn't match her sad eyes.

I knew I'd pushed her hard enough, so I saved the next question until after dinner on Monday.

"Can Dad come to DeAndre's birthday celebration too?" I said. More like yelled, because the noisy box fan was blowing and Mom was over by the sink.

Mom wrung the rag she was washing windows with and stared into the backyard. "I don't think your father will be able to make it."

"Well, I'll call and ask."

She shook her head slightly. "Please don't do that, sweetheart."

I gripped the side of the table. "How can we know whether he can come or not if we don't ask?"

She wrung the rag again, but no water came out. "It's complicated."

"No, it's not." Now I was yelling at the top of my lungs, and not because of the box fan. My words felt like hot lava bubbling up from my chest. "DeAndre was his son every bit as much as yours. He should be invited too."

Mom closed her eyes and dropped the rag in the sink. I braced myself for the reaction—for her to cry or yell or send me to my room. But she said nothing. For about two hours. It was the loudest silence I have ever heard.

Right before bed, Mom came into my room while

I was sewing some white lace onto the sleeves of a dress I'm working on. Her voice was cold. "I just spoke to your father. He says he'll be here next Wednesday for the birthday celebration. Good night."

I pushed my needle through the cloth without looking up. "Good night."

My chest felt tight, and I didn't know if it was because I was excited or sad or angry. Mom obviously didn't want to see Dad and I guilted her into it. Why did she have to make it such a big deal?

My parents are such drama. And Jack thinks *his* are unfair just because they took his phone away.

I'd give up my phone a million times over just for my parents to be together again.

Mario:

I worked for three hours on my "Why Mario Deserves a Smartphone" presentation. Three hours of research, formatting, finding images, summarizing bullet points. That's longer than I've worked for any school presentation. If this were for a class, I'd definitely get an A.

Our family computer is stationed in the living room,

Mario

so it was hard to keep the slideshow a secret. I worked on it a little here and there whenever everyone was gone. On Sunday, I waited until my parents put the twins to bed, and then I asked if I could show them my presentation.

I hooked the monitor up to the television and had them sit on the couch. The opening slide filled the TV screen: "The Benefits of Smartphone Ownership on Adolescents." I thought that sounded pretty professional, but Mom's grimace told me things weren't going to go well.

And they didn't.

A few seconds after my last slide, Mom pinched her lips together and gave Dad a look that said, "I'll take it from here."

She sighed. "Honey, I can tell you worked really hard on this. It was very well put together. But while you were researching, didn't you come across information from the other side of the argument?"

"Some," I admitted. "But that's not the point of this presentation."

"One of your points was that I'd be better able to communicate with you. But we can communicate just fine through your watch."

"Yeah, but I can't *do* anything on my watch." My heart pounded angrily.

"You can tell the time and send preset texts," Dad said. "That's all you need."

It was like they didn't hear anything I just said about social integration. In the end, they said we could talk about it again when I start driving. Driving! That's in, like, three years! Why are they so unreasonable?

Later that night, I called Tío Antonio to vent about everything that happened. Like always, he understood. He said my parents are trying to do what they think is best for me, and that I'll always be their baby, no matter how old I am. Well, I'm sick of being treated like a baby. I don't want them to feel like they have to protect me.

That's why I can't tell Mom about what happened after school yesterday, even though part of me wants to.

My week of being grounded was up, so Mom let me go to Perry's. As usual, he wanted to play video games in his room. (He's so lucky he's got a big-screen TV in there.)

"My cousin gave me all these," he said, holding up a stack of games. "I'll let you pick one."

I thought it was nice he was at least letting me pick the game. I chose a fantasy role-play game where the characters were dragon hunters.

We propped ourselves against his headboard with pillows behind our backs. Our characters approached a castle and a woman on horseback explained our mission.

This game was bloodier than ones we've played in the past. I'm not into gory stuff, but it looked pretty fake, so I pushed through it. The story line was interesting enough. About fifteen minutes in, we got to this moonlit hut—some sort of overnight inn. We went inside and the owner started telling a backstory.

And. Well . . .

That's when something bad came on the screen. Something involving a man and a woman that I definitely wasn't ready to see yet. I don't want to get into the details. All I will say is that it made my ears and neck burn and my heart pound so loud I was sure Perry could hear it.

I looked away really quick. "Dude, what's up with this game?"

"Yeahhhh," he said, eyes glued to the screen. "Awkward." The cutscene ended, and a band of men charged the hut. One took me out with an arrow, a streak of red splattering across the screen.

"Hey, pay attention!" Perry said. "You're down to one life."

I set the controller on his bed. All of a sudden, I felt squirmy, like I was sitting on a pile of rocks. "I don't wanna play this anymore."

He went after a couple of bad guys with his sword. "It's rated *M* for mature. If something bothers you, just ignore it."

For a moment, I felt stupid. Maybe he was right and I need to grow up. But what I saw didn't feel "mature." It felt the opposite.

I don't know why that game bothered me so much more than it bothered Perry. But the one thing I did know was that I wanted to get out of there. I sent my mom a preset text from my smartwatch: "I'm ready to come home." She was there in six minutes.

If Mom knew about what happened, she'd give me her I-told-you-so look and say something about how technology is full of inappropriate content and blah blah blah.

Yeah, I'm never telling Mom.

But now it stinks because I don't feel like playing video games with Perry anymore, and that's all he ever wants to do. Is it even possible to find someone who doesn't only want to do what THEY want to do all the time?

I didn't go to speed friendshipping today. I'm done trying.

If there were a hacky sack club, maybe I would join.

Brielle:

After school today, each student council candidate met in room 304 to record our election speeches. We stood in front of a maroon-and-gold backdrop (Franklin colors!) and spoke to a giant camera. It was intimidating, but less so than it would have been speaking in front of a full auditorium, so I can't complain.

Brielle

I rewrote my speech three times before landing on what I wanted to say. In the first draft, I focused on my qualifications, but it sounded too braggy. In the second, I tried to channel my inner Jack and crack some jokes, but it felt forced. For my final version, I focused on what I want to accomplish as president—and that's changed a lot in the past couple of weeks, thanks to some new friends. Our first-period teachers are going to play the videos before we vote next Friday. I can't wait to see what everyone thinks.

Because of the recording, I couldn't make it to speed friendshipping. Strangely, I kind of missed it.

Speed friendshipping is totally not my thing. Talking to people I don't know, worrying about what they're thinking about me, trying to get them to like me? It's exhausting.

But I missed it. I missed the people. It's weird.

Part of it has to do with Mei-ling. She and I got paired up the past couple of weeks, and she's super sweet. Last week, she showed me photos from when she visited her grandparents in Taiwan. My favorite was taken from the Central Mountain Range. Pink flowers blossomed at the peak of a mountain over a sea of clouds. The definition of peace.

I wish I could travel halfway around the world. Our only trip this summer will be staying at a family friend's cabin in Park City. That's only, like, two hours away! Dad has started listening to some podcast about frugal living and now he's always lecturing Mom and me about how we need to "live within our means" and "pay off our debts." It's getting super old.

He wouldn't even let Mom buy me teeth whiteners, like that's any of his business. In my live tutorial the other day, I was teaching how to apply lip liner, and someone commented that I need to whiten my teeth. So rude, but I know it's true. My teeth aren't, like, coffee-stained yellow—I'm not even allowed to drink coffee—but they're not as white as the other makeup MyTubers out there. Plus, I was using coral lipstick, and everyone knows that warm undertones bring out the yellow in your teeth. I should've been using a shade like plum. It's so embarrassing.

Mei-ling had my back, though. She responded

to the commenter and said, "Why do you have to be like that? Her teeth are gorgeous!" That was *so* sweet. Not even Devyn stands up for me, and she's my best friend. At least, she's supposed to be.

Mei-ling is someone I'd like to be friends with. Maybe one day we'll hang out outside of speed friend-shipping. It happened with Jack. He's been dropping by our table during lunch almost every day now, which makes for good comic relief.

Yesterday he showed up with a handful of salt packets and challenged me to a game of table football.

"The salt packet is the football," he said, sitting across from me. "We take turns sliding it toward each other. The goal is to get it hanging halfway off the table. That's a touchdown, six points." He formed a finger goalpost, thumbs pressed together. "Then you go for a field goal for an extra point."

I put my empty sandwich bag into my lunch sack. "So *this* is why I always saw you and Zane flicking salt packets around."

His cheek flinched a little. "Yeah. Okay, rock paper scissors for who starts."

My rock beat his scissors. On my first turn, the packet

skidded to a stop halfway across the table. "So, why do you never sit with him anymore?"

Jack looked confused. "Who?"

"Zane."

"Oh. Right." He crouched on the bench to get a better sliding angle. "I guess he just couldn't handle my awesomeness." He slid the packet and it flew off the edge, disappearing under the next table over.

"That stinks," I said.

"It's not a big deal. Everyone ditches me. They're threatened by my internet fame."

I snorted. "I was talking about the salt packet, but okay."

Jack scored the first touchdown (followed by his "uh-huh, oh, yeah" victory dance), but I came back with two in a row. Jack slapped the table in defeat, nearly knocking over Devyn's vitamin water. She left pretty immediately for the bathroom after that, taking Shawna and Lyla with her.

Once my friends were out of earshot, I paused before my turn. "Hey, you were kidding when you said everyone ditches you, right?"

"No, I was dead serious," Jack said in a very not-dead-serious tone. "You'll ditch me too. Give it a couple of weeks."

"Jack! What do you mean? That's a terrible thing to say."

"I kid, I kid." He laughed uncomfortably and brought his thumbs together in front of his face. "Field-goal time. Go for it."

He obviously didn't want elaborate on the ditching comment, so I took aim and flicked. The salt packet sailed through his fingers right as the bell rang. I cheered and leapt into the air, not worried about how weird I probably looked. Something about being with Jack makes you forget that other people are around.

Jack offered me his Starbursts as a prize, but I had to decline. Too sugary. I told him he should think of something else, and he agreed. Maybe he'll bring it to our meetup on Saturday. We have plans to make another collab video in the park, and I'm thinking we could do another table-football competition, except whoever loses has to take a shot of vinegar. I got that last part from a Paxton Poker video. I've been watching more of him since that's where Jack says he gets his inspiration.

Oh, yeah, that Paxton Poker guy even commented on our clothespin video and followed me! Jack's going to freak!

16

Tutor Time

Mom drives me to Tasha's on Saturday morning. At the stoplight, she beams at me from behind her extra-large sunglasses. "I'm so proud of you for finding yourself a tutor!" she says for probably the third time today. I can feel it: my sweet, precious phone and I are mere days from reuniting.

I ask Mom to stop by the 7-Eleven so I can grab a Slurpee as my tutoring fee. They're out of the cherry flavor, so I get razzleberry and hope it's close enough. What does *razzleberry* mean, anyway? Now that question is gonna haunt me and I can't even Google it.

Back on the road, Mom's GPS takes us into a neighborhood I've never been through before. The houses are older, the lawns are green, and the trees are huge, their shade blanketing the streets. "Your destination is on the right," Mom's phone says. "One thirteen West Orange Street."

Tasha's house sits partially hidden behind a couple of trees that look perfect for climbing. A brick chimney snakes up the side of the house, and the paneling is painted blue.

Mom parks. "Guess this is it. Have fun. Focus! Call me when you want to be picked up." She hands me the blocky pay-by-the-minute phone Dad got for me at Walmart.

I refuse to touch that thing. "I have your number memorized. I'll call you from Tasha's phone."

She tucks the atrocity into her purse. "If you insist."

As I walk up the concrete pathway, I get a strange feeling I'm forgetting something. I've got the Slurpee, and I'm fairly certain this is the time we set up. I'm probably just paranoid. I ring the doorbell but hear no sound. Maybe it's broken. I knock instead.

A woman with a friendly smile opens the door. She has warm brown eyes and skin just a shade darker than Tasha's. Her hair is tied back with a baby-blue bandanna, and sweat beads on her forehead.

"You must be Jack. I'm Trina." She motions inside. "Come on in."

The house is warm and somehow cozy, even though it's being renovated. The colorful rug in the entryway reminds me of my grandma's house. Down the hall, the baseboards are taped off with masking tape, and different shades of gray and beige stripe the walls. I duck under a ladder to pass into the living room. Don't people say walking under a ladder is bad luck? Hopefully it's not true.

Trina shows me her palms, which are speckled with dry plaster. "I'd shake your hand, but mine are dirty."

I shake her hand anyway. "No worries. I play in the mud all the time."

"You're a little charmer, aren't you?" She laughs and calls upstairs. "Tasha, your friend's here!"

A door creaks open and Tasha peeks out. She's not wearing her hat, and her hair reminds me of when Mom would buzz my head every summer when I was a kid. I focus on the paint stripes, feeling like I saw something I wasn't supposed to.

Tasha disappears back into her room, and when she comes back out, she's got a strawberry-colored hat on.

She takes a few steps down the stairs. "Hey. I'd say we could study at the kitchen table, but . . ." She points at the table, which sits crookedly between the living room and the kitchen island. It's covered with tools, brushes, and plastic sheeting. "Upstairs might be better. There's a family area."

"Cool." I walk up the stairs carefully so I won't trip and spill the Slurpee.

"Call out if you need drinks or anything," Trina says as she pushes the ladder to the wall.

"Thanks," I call over the balcony.

The open area at the top of the stairs has a brown leather couch with a coffee table in front of it. A stack of DVDs towers next to the TV, and a sewing machine sits on a desk in the corner with some clothes piled nearby and a dress hung over the top. On the wall hangs a single picture of Tasha and an older teenage boy, who I can only guess is her brother who passed away.

Tasha straightens the DVD stack. "Sorry my house is a mess. I tried to warn you."

"It's not that bad. At least it smells nice."

She scrunches her nose. "It smells like paint and sawdust."

"Yeah. Both nice things." I hold out the Slurpee. "Your payment."

She grabs it and takes a sip. "Mmm. Raspberry?"

"Razzleberry. They were out of cherry. Wait, is *razzleberry* just a fancy way to say *raspberry*?"

"No clue."

"Huh. It remains a mystery."

Tasha opens a thick binder and sits on the floor in front of the coffee table. "Did you bring a calculator?"

Maybe that's what I felt I was forgetting earlier. "Uh . . . no."

"What about notes?"

I shove my hands in my pockets. "I don't take notes. Unless you count doodles."

She gives me "the look" that moms give right before they send you to your room.

"I'm sorry!" I say. "But you can spot me, right?"

She laughs. "Yeah, I got notes. You should start taking them, you know. It'll help you remember what the teacher's saying."

"It's just so boring." I sit down opposite her in front of the coffee table.

"Class is more boring if you don't get what's going on," she says, handing me a pencil and a piece of paper. "All right. First let's figure out what grade you need on this test. It'll be good to have a goal in mind."

"You think we can figure that out? Is there some magic grade-calculating app that I'm unaware of?"

"We can use math. I guess that's kind of like magic." Tasha clicks open her binder rings and takes out the syllabus we got at the beginning of the year. I didn't know people actually kept those things.

"It says here how our grades are determined each semester." There are different percentages given to four sections: the final (20%), tests/quizzes (25%), homework (25%), classwork/citizenship (30%).

She writes an equation and makes me look up my grades on her phone through the school's student portal. She plugs my grade for each category into the equation.

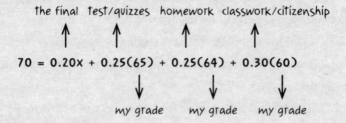

the final   test/quizzes   homework   classwork/citizenship

$$70 = 0.20x + 0.25(65) + 0.25(64) + 0.30(60)$$

my grade   my grade   my grade

An equation like this would normally make my brain shut off like an overheated laptop, but as she explains what each part means, something clicks. This must be the "light-bulb moment" I always hear people talking about.

"So x will be the grade I have to earn on the final to get a 70 percent in the class?"

"Exactly." She hands me her calculator. "Why don't you solve for x?"

I stare blankly at the calculator and can feel the wheels in my brain crank to a stop. The light bulb has flickered off again.

"Just start doing something. If you make a mistake, that's good. It'll help you remember what *not* to do."

"I don't even know where to start. Let's go help your mom paint."

"No! Start by multiplying 65 by 0.25. I know you know how to do that."

Slowly I tackle the equation. At one point, I add a number

to 70 I was supposed to subtract, and it comes out saying I need an 840 percent on my final to get a C in the class.

I rub my temples. "If that's right, I'm doomed."

Tasha shows me where I made the mistake, and I try again.

The second time I solve for x, it says I need to score 98.75 percent.

"That's right!" She high-fives me.

At first I'm ecstatic I found a number that makes sense. Then it sinks in. I can't earn this grade. That's impossible.

I push myself up from the table and act like I'm leaving. "Peace out, Tasha. We had a good run, but that's never gonna happen."

"Oh, stop being so dramatic. Ms. Snyder always puts, like, five extra-credit questions at the end of the test. It's doable."

"Says the girl who gets straight A's! I don't think I've gotten over a 90 percent in my life."

That's not true. I got a 94 percent last month on an English presentation where I collected music clips to show examples of metaphors in pop songs. But that was fun, so it doesn't count as schoolwork.

Tasha points to the equation I just solved. "This is exactly the kind of material that will be on the final. You can do this. The biggest problem was that you kept trying to give up."

"Wait, *this* is what's going to be on the test?"

"Yeah. We've been solving for x for, like, the past three weeks. Haven't you been paying attention?"

"No."

"That's your problem. Pay attention on Monday and Tuesday. Ms. Snyder said we're reviewing everything we learned this semester. Force yourself to listen!"

Easier said than done.

She looks over the equation again. "Also, your classwork and citizenship grades are pretty low. If you do the class worksheets and don't make smart-alecky comments, you're basically guaranteed full points for the day. A few days of 100 percent on citizenship will make a huge difference."

She's talking about this like it's actually possible, and the hope is starting to rub off on me. "You really think I can get up to a C by the end of the week?"

"I do." She reaches for the Slurpee to take a sip, and I notice that the pom-poms on her sleeves match the bottom of the dress by the sewing machine.

"These things, by the way," I say, batting at the pom-poms. "Do you sew them on yourself?"

"Yeah." She squishes one of the blue puffs. "They're kind of my trademark. I try to incorporate them into all my outfits."

"Do you make all your clothes?"

"I don't really *make* them. I just piece things together. It's kind of a hobby."

I point to the pile of clothes by the sewing machine. "Can I look at some of those?"

She raises an eyebrow. "Are you trying to avoid studying?"

"No! I really wanna see them."

She stands. "Fine. Just for a minute." She carefully lifts the dress off the sewing machine and holds it in front of her. It's white, a little boxy, and goes down to her knees. Dozens of mini pom-poms dangle at the bottom. "This piece is inspired by the flapper dresses of the thirties, but with a modern vibe, and thicker fabric."

I have no idea what she just said, but it sounds legit. "Are you gonna wear it to school?"

"No. I would never. I mean, I could, but it's too formal for me. I'm actually submitting a picture of this to a teen designer competition next week. It's hosted on MyTube."

"Sweet! I bet you'll win."

"Nah." She digs through the pile of clothes. "I'm an amateur. Some people are way more intense. I just get stuff from the thrift store and try to be creative."

She holds an orange shirt in one hand and a golden scarf in the other. "Like, I'm going to turn this scarf into sheer cap sleeves for this tube top."

"That'll look good." Whatever that means.

"Yeah. Some things you'd never think would go together make the most interesting combos." She puts the shirt back into the clothes pile. "Now, back to work. We can't afford to waste time."

We study for a solid twenty minutes longer, and things start making more sense. We review fractions and decimals, which are easier to deal with when I think of them in terms of grades. (Like, 7/10 is 0.7, or 70 percent. Why did I never realize that?) I even solve a word problem, and those are my nemesis. Eventually my stomach starts growling, and I decide it's time to go home for lunch. Tasha lets me use her phone to text Mom, and we study until she rings the doorbell.

"If you want, you can come over again next week," Tasha says as she walks me downstairs. "You'd have to bring your own notes, though."

Taking notes is totally not my style, but it's worth a shot. Especially if it means getting my citizenship grade up, which apparently counts for more than I realized. "I'll try to take notes. 'Try' being the key word."

We reach the bottom of the stairs, and I nod at Tasha. "I'll see you at school, I guess."

"Yep. I'll see ya."

"Thanks for everything," I say, my hand on the doorknob. "It's really nice of you to be helping me like this."

She smiles and turns to walk upstairs. "I'm just in it for the Slurpees."

I'll have to get her an extra-large one next time.

17

Another One
Bites the Dust

In math on Monday, I ask Ms. Snyder if I can move to the front row.

"Why is that?" she asks with an arched eyebrow. I wonder if she heard about my marshmallow darts and suspects I want to get a close aim at her.

"I want to be able to focus."

She pinches her lips together like she tasted something sour. I haven't given her much reason to trust me. How can I prove I'm legit?

I pull out my notebook and open to my study notes from last night. I didn't want to forget what I practiced at Tasha's, so I made up some equations and practiced solving for x a few times on my own. "Look. I've even been study-ing. I really want to do well on this final and raise my grade to a C."

She nods slowly as reviews my work. I'm afraid she's go-ing to point out a mistake I made, but she doesn't. "If you can get someone to switch seats with you, that's fine. We'll have our last seating change next week, and I'll make sure you're in the front row."

I almost say, "No! Don't move me permanently!" I want to sit in the front today and tomorrow only. Once I get my grade up, I won't need to try as hard. But since I'm trying to get full citizenship points this week, I don't think that com-ment would help.

"Thanks, Ms. Snyder!" I clasp my hands together. "You're the bestest and fairest math teacher in all the land." I could swear she almost smiles.

The guy I ask to switch seats with seems eager to take my spot near the back. Everyone knows that the kids in the front never get away with closing their eyes or sneaking a glance at their phones or anything. At least there are only a few weeks left of school. I don't think I could handle being a front-row kid for much longer than that.

The nice thing about sitting in front is that I don't have to get up if I want to say something to Ms. Snyder. "Hey," I say from my new desk, which is right by hers. "If I'm really good today, will you email my parents and tell them?"

"I should have known this was about getting out of trouble." She smirks. "Sure. If you behave well all week, I'll email your parents. But that means no outbursts. And no irrelevant comments."

That sounds hard. "What if they aren't completely relevant, but I raise my hand first?"

"You may make one irrelevant comment per day."

I nod. With only one, I'd better make it good.

During class, I take as many notes as I can, but it's hard because I'm not the fastest writer. I'm so busy scribbling stuff down that I even forget to make my one irrelevant comment. A lot of what Ms. Snyder talks about is stuff I went over at Tasha's house. Most of it makes sense, surprisingly. I even write down one of the questions I didn't understand to ask Tasha about later.

Something about taking notes makes class go by faster than usual. I'm shocked when the bell rings and check the clock to make sure it wasn't a mistake.

I stop at Ms. Snyder's desk on my way out and hold up my notebook. "Look at all my notes! I filled up, like, two whole pages!" She peers over her glasses. "Well done. Make sure you study at home."

"I will! I'm totally acing this test!" If she sees how important this is to me, then maybe she'll be more lenient when grading. I'll even throw in a doodle of her as a math-themed superhero at the bottom of my test. Worth a shot.

I studied on Monday night, but I didn't get far. Mom was watching *Weeks of Our Lives* in the living room and I had to find out the fate of Fabio and Suzanne—guilty as charged. I know that if I study with Tasha again, I'll be forced to focus. So, at the end of the lunch period on Tuesday, I head to her table. On the way over, I wave to Brielle, but strangely, she doesn't wave back. Instead, she frowns, stands and walks straight out of the room.

What was that all about? Did she have to use the bathroom? Brielle's friends are all still at the table, so I take a detour to talk with them. Maybe they know what's up.

"Where'd Brielle go?" I ask Devyn.

She sweeps her hair over her shoulder. "I don't know. She's mad at you for not showing up at the park on Saturday."

The park! Shoot! THAT is what I felt like I was forgetting. We were supposed to make a video together! I imagine her sitting all alone on the park bench, frowning and checking the time. It makes me sick to my stomach.

"Will you tell her I'm sorry?"

"Uh-huh, sure," Devyn says in a way that tells me she really won't. I'll have to apologize to Brielle myself.

Or maybe it'd be safer to hold off for a day or so until she forgets about it. Brielle looked pretty angry leaving the cafeteria. What if she chews me out in the hallway the same way Zane did a couple of weeks ago?

Yeah. Avoiding her would probably be the smartest. At least for now.

I head to Tasha's table for the last two minutes of lunch. I recognize a couple of the girls she sits with—Kayla and Jeanette. They always convince our science teacher to let them sit by each other since they behave well in class.

"What up, mathmagician?" I say to Tasha. Her friends give me confused smiles.

I lean my elbows on the table. "Does the offer still stand to come over this week? How about after school?"

Her friends exchange glances. They obviously had no idea Tasha and I know each other. Is she embarrassed we hung out or something?

I guess we didn't really "hang out." I paid her a Slurpee to tutor me. Not anything worth mentioning.

Tasha pulls one side of her hat over her ear. "I still have to submit to that MyTube contest, so maybe a little later? Like four?"

"Ah, yeah!" I look at Kayla and Jeanette. "Have you guys seen her fashion designs? She's got this contest in the bag, right?"

Kayla looks at Tasha. "You make fashion designs?"

Tasha bites her lip and looks down. "Uh, yeah. Kind of."

That's weird. Everyone at speed friendshipping knows she's into fashion. She doesn't exactly try to hide it.

Tasha crinkles up her lunch sack. "I might not be able to tutor for long. I have to do some prep for a celebration we're having at my house tomorrow. But we'll cram in as much as we can."

"A party? With food? I'm invited, right?"

She laughs awkwardly. "It's . . . kind of a family thing."

"I'm just kidding." I stand to leave. "But yeah, I'll be there right at four o'clock so we can get as much done as possible!"

I'm not there right at four. When I was picking up Tasha's Slurpee at the 7-Eleven, the nacho cheese machine glitched and exploded orange goop all over the floor. Like, three dunderheads walked right through the cheese puddle.

One of them may or may not have been me.

Mom made me wrap my tennis shoes in a grocery bag and drove me home to switch into sandals.

I get to Tasha's closer to four-fifteen. She answers the door, and her mom calls, "Hi, Jack!" from the kitchen between drilling sounds.

"Hey, Trina!" I hand Tasha the Slurpee. "Extra-large. They had cherry today."

"My favorite," she says, and takes a sip.

As we walk up the stairs, I realize that the walls are now painted beige, and the tape has been taken off the baseboards. "The house is looking nice."

"It's coming together."

Upstairs, I set my backpack on the couch and pull my notes out. "I hope we have time to go over everything. Sorry I'm late."

"It's fine. I was running late too. I just finished the final touches on my dress and was about to take pictures of it." She sets her drink on the coffee table and grabs the boxy white dress. She's added some rows of tan beads to the neckline.

She steps forward and sweeps the dress in front of her. "What do you think?"

"Looks great! I like these." I lean over the table to feel the beads, but my knee hits the Slurpee. My heart stops as the cup topples to its side. I reach out, but it's too late: red slush gushes off the side of the table, drenching the bottom of the dress.

Tasha gasps, and her eyes pop out like she's a squeezy toy.

"Oh no, oh no, oh no!" I say. I grab my head, which I have the sudden urge to bang on the coffee table. "I'm so sorry. Can we fix it? Will it wash out?"

She lays the dress on the couch and examines the damage while clenching the top of her hat. If she had hair, I bet she'd be pulling it.

"The deadline to submit is in"—she checks her phone—"thirty minutes. Maybe if we found some bleach and a hair dryer." She darts downstairs, clutching the dress in one hand, and yells, "Mom, where is the bleach?"

My stomach feels like a wet rag being rung out over and over. I follow downstairs, hoping to help in any way I can.

Trina can't find any bleach, so she drives to the store to get some. Under Tasha's direction, I rinse the stain in the kitchen sink while she rummages through the cupboards in hopes of finding stain remover. "Why can I never find anything in this house?" she sputters, pulling out random cleaning supplies onto the floor. I've never seen her frustrated before. She's usually so calm.

I turn off the faucet. The red stain still stands out against the white fabric. "Maybe you can explain what happened," I say weakly. "Like, 'this dumb guy spilled a Slurpee on this right before I took its picture.' It might make you stand out."

"I'm not sure that's the best way to stand out. It'd be unprofessional."

"I could remove the stain with Photoshop."

She shakes her head. "If they notice, I'd get disqualified." She checks the oven clock. "My mom'll never get back in time. I'll have to submit something else."

We go upstairs and rummage through the clothes pile by the sewing machine. I help her pick another outfit: a green shirt with triangle-patterned fabric and a brown crocheted neckline. It's cool, but not as detailed as the one I ruined.

"I wish I could make this up to you," I say. "I feel awful."

She frowns. "Don't beat yourself up, Jack. Accidents happen."

"They seem to happen to me more often than to your average human."

Tasha collapses onto the couch. "Honestly, I wasn't going to win anyway. At least I have a backup outfit." She checks her phone. "You should probably tell your mom to pick you up now. I've gotta submit this soon, and I need to touch it up. Then I gotta bleach the other dress when my mom gets home and get it into the wash before the stain sets in."

I text Mom on Tasha's phone and wait on the couch while she sews brown pom-poms onto the sleeves of the green shirt. When the doorbell rings, I grab my backpack. "Well, I'll see you tomorrow, I guess."

"Sorry we didn't get to study."

"That's my fault, not yours."

Tasha pushes her needle back into a tomato-shaped

pin cushion. "I saw you taking lots of notes in class. Review them with your parents. You'll be fine."

"Yeah. You're probably right." Biggest lie of my life.

On the car ride home, Mom asks how studying went. I say it went well. No need to rehash everything. She asks if I'm going back again, and I say I'm not sure. The truth is, I've never been more sure of anything: Tasha will never invite me back again. And who could blame her? Being a fashion designer is her biggest passion, and I ruined her chances at a contest she seemed excited about.

And another one down, and another one down, and another friend bites the dust.

In the course of about two weeks, I've managed to annoy Zane, Mario, Brielle, and now Tasha. I always thought my friendships didn't last because the other person was flaky, or boring. But the more I hang out with people, the more it becomes clear. Everything is always my fault.

At this point, why bother looking for a talent show partner? I'll tell Ms. Campbell tomorrow: I'm dropping out.

18

Reunited, and
It Feels So Good

In math on Wednesday, I come prepared. I've got a pencil in one hand and a green squishy pig in the other. Mom bought me the squishy pig, which is technically a stress toy. She read that they can help you stay calm and focused during tests. I showed it to Ms. Snyder at the beginning of class, and (after making sure it didn't squeak) she said that as long as I didn't throw it or make it a distraction, I could use it.

It's more important than ever before that I get my phone back. It's all I have left. I miss talking to my friends online. I miss how they're always there. I miss being able to post stuff and laugh at videos and make funny comments. Real life has been a drag lately.

Last night, I asked Dad to help me study, and he was more than enthusiastic. He didn't remember how to do a couple of the equations, so we called in Jacob, who knew exactly what to do. I guess that's one perk of having a genius brother.

I stare at the first question on the final and crack my knuckles. It's a word problem that has to do with percentages. I use Tasha's trick and circle all the numbers first. Then I reread the question twice. I write an equation based on the numbers, and I think I get it right. It felt a little too easy, which I'm not sure is a good sign.

I squeeze my pig a few times and breathe deeply. It will be okay.

During the last fifteen minutes of class, everyone starts finishing. My heartbeat ticks up a notch with each person who turns in their test. Soon I realize I'm the only person still working. I probably look so stupid. I bet everyone wishes I'd finish so Ms. Snyder would give us free time. But I still have five extra-credit questions, and then I need to go back and review as many of my answers as possible. I squeeze my pig so hard, I'm sure he'd squeal if he could. Turning in my test early never worked out for me before, so I might as well use every second to my advantage.

The bell rings when I'm about three-quarters of the way through checking my answers. Everyone leaves, but I stay put to finish the problem I'm reviewing. A minute later, I walk up to Ms. Snyder's desk and hand her the test. "Can you grade it now? Please?"

She places the test on top of a huge stack. "I'll post the grades on the student portal after school."

"Oh, Ms. Snyder," I beg, "I don't think I can wait that long! The suspense will kill me!"

She puts her elbows on her desk and taps the tips of her fingers together. "If anyone knew I graded yours first, they would think I gave you special treatment."

"I won't tell anyone. I swear."

She removes her glasses and wipes them on her sleeve. "I'll tell you what. I have my preparation period right now. Come by after your next class, and I'll let you know what you got."

"Thank you! Thank you! I worship at your feet!" I press my hands together and bow deeply. I'd give her a hug, but I have a feeling that wouldn't go over well.

Her eyes crinkle and she laughs a little. "Get to your next class before you're late."

It's hard to focus during my next period, but I make extra use of my squishy pig. When the bell rings, I run to math. Ms. Snyder's eyes gleam as she slowly raises my test. At the top, in big, red ink numbers, it says 98.8%.

I gasp and freeze with my mouth hanging open. If Josh were here, he'd probably start throwing grapes in my mouth. As the reality sinks in, I start bouncing, and then hopping, and then straight-up jumping into the air.

Ms. Snyder chuckles. "Calm down, kangaroo."

She hands me the test, and I flip through the pages. "I even got three of the five extra-credit questions right!"

Ms. Snyder leans back in her chair. "So Jack has a knack for math. Too bad we didn't know this earlier."

After school, Mom's so impressed with my score that she hangs my test on the refrigerator like I'm in kindergarten again, but I don't even care. When I show her that my grade on the student portal is now a 70.1 percent, she checks with Dad and then hands me my phone. I'm so happy, I can barely listen while she reviews the new rules about turning it in before dinner and setting app limits and stuff like that. I nod vigorously and then grab my test off the fridge. I dash to my room, ready to post my first video in two weeks.

I back-flop onto my bed and start recording. *"Guess who's baaaaack?"* I sing. "You've missed me, right? I've been grounded from my phone the past couple of weeks, but then *this* happened." I hold up my test. "How 'bout that? Ninety-eight percent, baby! Never getting rid of me now!" I do my famous head-bop happy dance before signing off with, "Gotta run."

Immediately the comments pile up. Everyone's shocked that I got such a high grade.

"I got a C on that final, dude!" says Max Hutchinson.

"Well done, Jack," says Mei-ling from speed friendshipping.

"How'd you cheat?" says this guy I barely know. "I need tips!"

I almost reply that I got study help from Tasha, but I figure she wouldn't want to be associated with me after I ruined her dress. She didn't even tell her best friends she was tutoring me.

I check my personal page and see the countdown I put up in the corner. "Three days till talent show!" it says. In first period, I told Ms. Campbell I was dropping out, so I delete the countdown and hope no one notices. It's too bad. The food challenge would have been epic. Ms. Campbell did say to let her know if I change my mind. Maybe I'll break down and ask Michael Lee to be my assistant. I'd probably end up ruining his life by accident, though.

I go to Brielle's page to check how many views we're up to on our clothespin video. When I see the number, my jaw drops. Holy guacamole! We're nearing eleven thousand! I've become practically internet famous and didn't even know it.

I look at the reactions, and when I see the most-liked comment on top, my jaw doesn't just drop—it practically detaches from my face.

"Oh, man, classic! Can't wait to see what you guys come up with next. Subscribing to you both."

And the author of the comment? The one that—yes, I can confirm—subscribed to my account?

Paxton. Freaking. Poker.

The next day, I catch Brielle in the halls after English. I had to practically chase her out the door because she left so fast. She's been doing that a lot lately, so I haven't been able to apologize for accidentally standing her up at the park. Hopefully we can smooth things over, because I'm starting to miss her. Plus, we *have* to make another video. We've kept Paxton waiting long enough. (I think we're on a first-name basis now, right?)

I nudge her shoulder. "Dude!"

She keeps walking. "Don't call me dude."

"Sorry. Dudette?"

"Even worse."

I step in front of her. "Look. If this is about the park,

I'm really sorry. I was studying with Tasha and forgot to show up."

She uses her binder to push me out of the way. "I saw you got your phone back." That's not a response to my apology, but at least she's making conversation.

"Yeah! Aced my math test."

"Well, now you can make your own videos. You don't need me." She walks faster.

I trail behind. "Why are you being like this? I said I was sorry! Haven't you ever forgotten about plans you made?"

"No."

I should've called that one. "Well, not everyone's as perfect as you, Brielle."

She spins toward me with wide, angry eyes. I know I struck a nerve. "Do you think I'm stupid?" she says quietly. "Your timing's too obvious. You're only apologizing because you saw that Poker-what's-his-face commented on our video."

"Well, you've *kind of* been avoiding me, so it's not my fault I couldn't say sorry sooner."

"It's not just that. You blew me off to study because getting your phone back was more important than following through with our plans. You use people when it benefits you."

I swallow hard. That's not true. "I said I'm sorry. What more can I do?"

"You're not acting sorry."

"Oh, my bad. Would you like me to cry?" I fake-sob and wipe invisible tears.

She rolls her eyes. "Yeah, real mature," she says coldly before walking away. "You're so annoying. No wonder your friends always end up ditching you."

This time, I don't follow her. Instead I stand and glare at the back of her head. That was a low blow. I should never have told her about my friends ditching me. I should never have let her know it bothered me. What was I thinking?

Brielle's halfway down the hall, but her last words still hover in the air, pricking at my skin like Tasha's sewing needles. If she thinks I'm so annoying, maybe I should prove her right. I want so badly to call out something mean, like tell her she's boring, or stuck up, or something *she's* self-conscious about. But I can't bring myself to do it, and I don't know why.

The two-minute warning bell rings, reminding me I need to get to science. I turn the corner and see Zane by the drinking fountain. I don't feel like dealing with whatever snarky comment he's bound to throw at me as I pass.

Zane catches my eye and calls out, "Hey, Jack! What's up?" He sounds friendly, but it's probably a trap, like he's gonna walk up to me and stick gum in my hair or something. I speed up and veer toward the other end of the hall.

Zane weaves through the crowded hall to catch up with me. "Where you headed?"

I keep my pace. "Science. I'm running late."

"Like you care about being late, right? Ha!" He jabs me with his elbow. "Hey, so I heard Paxton Poker commented on that clothespin video you made. That's so sweet, man!"

Now I get it. Anything Paxton Poker considers cool becomes cool. I guess I'm friendworthy again.

"When are you gonna drop your next video?" Zane asks. "Do you and Brielle have something planned?"

"Not anymore. She's mad at me."

"What for?"

"I don't know. Some dumb reason."

"Not surprised. She gets mad about everything."

I bet he's thinking about his sixth-grade pool party when he shot Brielle in the back of the head with a water gun and she told his mom. They've never liked each other since.

"It kind of kills me that the video you guys made got more views than our T-rexing one," Zane says. "Remember how that lady in the flower aisle freaked out when you ran past her?" He jumps and clutches his chest.

I can't help but snort. "That was hilarious. Too bad no one T-rexes anymore."

"Maybe we can make another video sometime. It's been forever."

I don't point out that it's been forever because of *him*. I know he just wants to make videos again because he knows Paxton Poker will see them.

If so, he's doing the same thing Brielle called me out for. I can't blame him.

As pathetic as it sounds, it's kind of nice to have Zane talking to me again. If I try really hard not to annoy him, things could go back to the way they were.

I shrug. "You can come over today if you want."

"Yeah, totally!" We approach my classroom, and he waves to someone down the hall. "I'll text you after school," he says, walking backward toward his friend.

Part of me is annoyed that Zane's acting like nothing happened and we're totally cool. I'm also annoyed with myself for letting him get away with it. But if Zane's the best I can do in the friendship arena, then so be it. I don't want to be like Brielle and hold on to a grudge.

Maybe Zane and I just needed a temporary break. It's not like I expected us to have a dramatic heart-to-heart apology session. Besides, I really need someone to help me with my future videos. If Paxton Poker likes them, he might share them with his massive audience and get me tons of followers. And once I reach Paxton Poker status, I won't need to worry about finding friends anymore. I'll have people begging to collab with me.

It's nice to imagine, anyway.

19

Stay Lovely

After school, Zane spins in my office chair, just like the good old days.

"The good old days" being about three weeks ago, if my math is correct.

I just finished telling him about how Brielle yelled at me for forgetting about the park, leaving out the details of her exact wording.

"Brielle's such a snob." Zane tosses my squishy pig in the air. "Imagine if she actually wins student body president tomorrow. She'll probably, like, ban marshmallows, or make homework mandatory."

I lean the back of my head against the couch's armrest.

"I don't think she even likes the student body. She just wants to be the leader because she loves telling people what to do."

"Yeah, like in English the other day, when she shushed everyone."

Brielle didn't really shush *everyone*. She shushed Zane and Jared. They were talking about "getting gains" while Ms. Campbell was finishing the second-to-last chapter of *The Outsiders*. At the time, I was glad Brielle got them to be quiet. It's hard to hear Ms. Campbell's voice from the back row.

"That was so weird," I agree anyway. I don't feel like defending Brielle ever again. "So, got any ideas for our next video?"

Zane pokes at the pig. "You're the mastermind. I'm just here to help."

"I've been trying, but I can't think of anything good. There's too much pressure knowing that Paxton Poker might see whatever we post."

"Yeah," Zane says. "It has to be extra good. Maybe you'll get to collab with him one day."

"I don't know. He lives in Ohio." I had the same thought and looked it up. MyTube stars often collaborate, but only if they both have big enough audiences.

Zane shrugs. "Anything's possible."

I'm glad at least one person is supportive of my MyTube career. The way Zane's acting, maybe he'd be down for doing the talent show again.

"I do have a cool talent show idea that might get his attention," I say slowly.

Zane's head perks up, so I pull my food dartboard out of my closet and explain my plan.

Zane listens quietly, looking over the different food sections. "I love it," he says when I finish. I wait for him to give some improvement suggestions like Mario did, but instead he just nods. "I'm in."

My heart does a quick somersault. Now I can tell Ms. Campbell that the show's back on! I try to mask my excitement so Zane doesn't think I was desperate without him.

I set the dartboard on my desk. "Sweet. Let's plan on meeting a half hour before the show to run through it."

"Sounds good."

"In the meantime, we really gotta post some stories so the algorithms don't work against us when we post the talent video."

He furrows his brows. "Algor-what?"

It feels good to be using a big word that Zane doesn't understand. "An algorithm is, like, the way a social network sorts your posts. If people don't interact with your account for a while, you'll stop showing up first on their feed."

"Ah, I think I knew that. What's something quick we could do?"

I think through the latest Paxton Poker stories I've watched. Lots of them are just him dancing. "Maybe we can invent a new dance move. We can post on our stories until it catches on."

"That could work." Zane rubs his chin. "How do you invent a dance move?"

"Easy. You just pick a random object and let it inspire you. Like, there was that kid a while back who made Flossing popular." I start to Floss. "Then there are the classics. The Shopping Cart." I pull groceries down into an imaginary cart. "Or the Cotton Swab." I pretend to clean my ears out and throw away the Q-tip.

Zane laughs and looks around my room. "The Clothes Hanger?" He fakes hanging up clothes to a beat.

"How about the Flyswatter," I say, and pretend to smack a fly on the wall.

"The Plunger?" He mimes plunging a toilet.

"Oh! Or we could go with the Toilet." I flush an imaginary toilet and rotate my hips like water swirling in the bowl.

Zane cracks up. "That's it! That's totally the one!"

He pulls out his phone and cranks up some rap song that comes on the radio a lot. We do the Toilet all around the room. I even get up on the couch and try to do the Toilet while jumping off.

This one's gonna make it big-time, I can tell. One day back with Zane and we're killing it. The dream team, together again.

After we upload our dancing clips to my story, Zane

starts scrolling through his feed and comes across Brielle's latest video.

"It's not fair," he says. "Brielle's always posts these boring makeup tutorials and gets a crap ton of views."

"Yeah," I agree. "Boring's her thing." I know it's not true, but I say it anyway. She's the one who made our mall video exciting. And I always looked forward to stopping by her lunch table because she was always down to goof around. But how can she refuse to forgive me, even after I said I was sorry?

Zane watches a few seconds of Brielle showing how to apply eye shadow. He mimics her high-pitched voice. *"Purple is so in this season."*

"You can't forget the humblebrag." I do the Brielle voice too. *"Some lady at the mall asked me if I was interested in modeling, but I'm so busy, I don't have time."*

He laughs. "You know what? We should make our own makeup tutorial. That'd be hilarious."

"Me? Put on makeup? I don't know how."

"That's why it would be funny. We could talk like Brielle and smear lipstick all over our faces or something."

I think of the act my cousins performed at our family-reunion talent show last summer. One person would stand behind someone else while feeding them different foods. The yogurt ended up slopped all over my cousin Jenna's face.

It was funny with food. It could work with makeup too.

"My mom keeps her makeup in her bathroom," I say. "I'm sure if we used a little, she wouldn't mind."

After a half hour of collecting materials, planning the script, and recording, Zane and I plop onto the couch to watch our finished product. I wipe the thick makeup off my face with a damp hand towel and press Play.

In the video, I'm sitting in my desk chair with my Transformers poster behind me. On my head is the same yellow mop wig I used for the spaghetti-slap video. It smelled even mustier than the last time I wore it, but what can I say? Beauty is sacrifice.

In front of me, a card table is set up with an assortment of Mom's makeup. I knew what blush, eye shadow, lipstick, and mascara were, but some of the other stuff we had to Google the names of—like concealer, which is the goopy tan stuff you smear on your face.

"Hello, dears," I say in a high-pitched, Brielle-inspired voice. She's the only makeup tutorialist I've seen, so I didn't have any other examples to go off of.

"Today I'm going to show you how to make yourselves gorgeous like me." I flip my mop hair over my shoulder. *"Not as gorgeous as me, obviously, but if you really try hard, you might come close.*

"First things first, let's start off with this magical goop stuff I like to call melted skin. It basically hides all your normal, gross skin so that you have newer, meltier skin."

As I'm talking, Zane (who's hiding behind me) dips his fingers into a little bowl we filled with concealer and spreads it thickly over my face. He accidentally gets a little on my lips, so I improvise by licking it off and trying to hide my disgust. *"Mmm. Tastes like chocolate.*

"Next is blush! The purpose of blush is to make yourself look embarrassed all the time. Everyone knows that the more embarrassed you look, the more gorgeous you are."

Zane overdoes the blush, and I end up looking like a sunburned clown.

"Time for eyeliner!"

During planning, I was terrified that Zane would poke me in the eye with this one, but we came up with a good solution:

"Eyeliner is essential. It shows the world where your eyes end and where your face begins!" Zane draws huge circles around my eyes so it looks like I'm wearing black glasses. *"The*

wider you go, the bigger your eyes will appear. We're going for the Disney princess look.

"Last is mascara! Long eyelashes are so last year. Instead use your mascara to create some nice beauty marks on your face."

Zane dabs three black splotches on each of my cheeks.

"No one will even know these are fake."

To finish, I purse my lips and run my hands through my mop hair. "The look is now complete, and It. Is. Perfection. Make sure to subscribe for more cutting-edge beauty tips." I flash a peace sign and say, "Stay lovely." That's how Brielle ends all her makeup tutorials.

I put my phone down on the couch and try to catch my breath. My stomach hurts from laughing. I knew while filming that I looked ridiculous, but I didn't realize the extent of it.

Zane has lost it too. "The blush part, though!" he says. He rolls off the couch and clunks to the floor.

"Do you think we need to edit anything?" I ask once we finally cool down.

"I don't think so. It's only a few minutes. Let's post it."

My finger hovers over the Publish button. Brielle is gonna hate this. I'm not sure it's something I want her to see.

"What if we cut the ending where I say 'Stay lovely,'" I suggest. "It's too obviously like Brielle. That's her signature phrase."

"Nah, that's the best part. Your impression is spot-on."

"But Brielle will know it's about her."

"So?"

Maybe he's right. Why do I care so much about Brielle's feelings? She doesn't care about mine. She verbally gut-punched me where she knew it would hurt. Maybe it's time she gets a taste of her own medicine.

"Trust me," Zane says. "This might be the best video you've ever made."

I ignore the little voice in my head and press Publish.

My stomach twists again, and, for the first time ever, I secretly hope this one doesn't get a lot of views.

20

Whose Fault Is It, Anyway?

After Zane goes home, I sneak all of Mom's makeup back into her bathroom. The only thing she might realize we used is the concealer since so much of it is gone. Hopefully that stuff isn't expensive.

When I check in on the video, it's taken off like a virus. People tag their friends and put crying-laughing emojis. "Best makeup tutorial I've seen all year," one comment says. Maybe no one will realize we're mocking Brielle.

"STAY LOVELY," another person says, followed by a puking emoji. Uh-oh. They definitely caught the reference.

Mom makes me turn in my phone before dinner, so at

night, I can't check the comments coming in. I toss and turn in bed so much that I think I'm gonna wear a hole in my pillowcase. What's Brielle gonna think when she sees the video? Will she scream at me in the hall? Or worse, never talk to me again?

The next day before English starts, Zane smacks his hand on my desk. "Dude, did you *see* who liked our video?" He holds up his phone to reveal Paxton Poker's name at the top of the screen. I should be ecstatic, but I can barely force a grin.

"We're totally on his radar," I say.

"I know! It's insane." He walks off to show off our newest fan to Jared. "You can't see me in the video, but the whole thing was my idea," I overhear Zane say. Psht. I'm the one who made it funny.

Maybe it's better if I let him take the credit.

I roll my pencil around the top of my desk and keep an eye on the door, waiting for Brielle to walk in and shoot laser eyes at me. My heart thumps each time the handle turns, but it's always someone else. This is weird. Brielle's never late. Maybe she's too afraid to show her face. What if she's at home crying?

People are laughing on the other end of the room, so I turn to see what's going on. Alex has an open tube of mascara in his hand and has drawn three beauty marks on each of his cheeks.

"Give it back," Cynthia says, reaching for the mascara. "You look beautiful enough."

The bell rings and the announcements click on over the loudspeaker. *"Happy Friday!"* says the voice. After reminding us about speed friendshipping and the talent show Saturday night, she says, *"Now it's time to vote for next year's student council representatives! Teachers, please distribute the ballots and play the pre-recorded speeches from our fabulous candidates. Vote wisely and have a wonderful day!"*

Ms. Campbell passes a stack of ballots down each aisle. "Please vote for only one candidate per category," the directions say, as if we couldn't figure that out ourselves. Ms. Campbell dims the lights and turns on the projector screen, and the room hushes.

First those running for treasurer give their speeches, which last about thirty seconds each. I vote for Max Hutchinson because he comments on my videos a lot. For secretary, I vote for Julia Miles, since she gave me a piece of gum in history once. I don't know any of the three vice presidential candidates, so I choose the person with the coolest name (Zelda Martinez).

Only two people are running for president: Zane and Brielle. Zane's clip is first.

He's got his hands in the pockets of his training pants, which I bet Mr. Busby would say makes him look like he doesn't care.

He flips his hair out of his eyes. *"What up, Franklin Middle? I'm Zane. Most of you know me. I wanna be your president because I wanna make lots of cool changes to this school. Like, I don't know, maybe cool assemblies where we pie teachers or something. My older brother did that when he went here. Anyway, if you vote for me, it'll be a party."* He points at the camera. *"Use your brain. Vote for Zane."* The camera cuts off.

Jared presses a fist to his mouth and, midcough, says, "Pick Zane." Ms. Campbell shushes him. "Vote in silence, please."

After a couple of seconds of a blank screen, Brielle's image appears. She sits up straight and stares directly into the camera. Her dark blue button-down shirt makes her look like she's at a job interview.

She takes a deep breath, like she always does when she's nervous.

"Hello. My name is Brielle Kimball, and I want to be your student body president. I love this school and hope to change it for the better.

"The past two weeks, I went to speed friendshipping after school. To be honest, I wasn't excited about it at first. I just thought it was something a student council candidate should do. But it ended up being really fun talking to people and learning about them. Like, Kevin's into baking. Mario's into hacky sack. Tasha's into fashion. It got me thinking . . . we need more clubs at this school. Places where people with similar interests

can hang out. Or even better, places where people can try new things. I definitely wouldn't be opposed to joining a baking club.

"Our school will be stronger if we have fun together. That's why during my term as president, I would focus on unity. The more we get to know each other, the more school can feel like home.

"Stay lovely, Franklin."

Several people snicker at those final words, a joke understood by everyone who saw my video. Brielle had no idea at the time of recording that her signature phrase would be turned into a mockery. All thanks to me. A couple of rows over, Jared quietly mimics Brielle's voice. "Stay lovely, Franklin!" I want to stand up and scream. That was a great speech. A little stiff, but at least it had substance. Zane only wants to be president because he likes feeling popular. Brielle actually wants to improve the school. Her club ideas are awesome.

I can't chew Jared out, though. I used the same "Brielle" voice in my MyTube video, so I have no room to talk. The puky feeling in my stomach makes me think I should just delete the stupid video altogether. But everyone would be bugging me about where it went, and Zane would think I was being dramatic. The damage has been done.

I look at my ballot, and a choice has never felt easier.

I check "Brielle Kimball."

At the beginning of sixth period, the class phone rings. Mr. Gus says a few words to whoever called, and hangs up.

"Jack. Come here, please."

A couple of kids sing *"Oooh"* as I walk to his desk. I have a sinking feeling I know what this is about.

Mr. Gus speaks softly, which is good since I bet the whole class is trying to eavesdrop. "Principal Duncan asked you to stop by his office during the last five minutes of class."

A wave of dread rushes over me. "Why can't I go now?"

"He has a meeting." He stands and walks to the whiteboard to begin class.

I groan and return to my seat. Now I'm gonna have to wait in suspense the whole period. This is definitely a form of cruel and unusual punishment. Principal Duncan seems to be fond of that. I bet the Table of Shame was his idea too.

Throughout the period, I can't pay attention to anything but the clock. The second hand has never ticked so slowly. It feels like the time I went to a football game with Dad: the countdown timer would say two minutes left, and then ten minutes later, it would say one minute left. I chew the eraser off my pencil without realizing what I'm doing. Maybe I'm just paranoid. This can't be about the video. I made it in the privacy of my own home. I can't get in trouble for that at school, right?

Brielle is Principal Duncan's pet, though. She's in charge of the service club, and she's always sucking up to him. I even heard her compliment his tie once. She could have told on me for revenge. I saw her at lunch, so I know she's not home sick. She kind of *looked* sick, though. Her hair was thrown into a ponytail, and she wore a baggy sweatshirt, which is unusual for her. At one point, Devyn put her arm around her and whispered something in her ear. I'm sure Devyn knows what's going on. Maybe she's the one who ratted me out.

I hide my phone under my desk and sneak a peek at Brielle's MyTube for any hints of how she's doing. She hasn't posted anything since yesterday's photo of the pizza slice she had for lunch. It looks gross. Pretty sure there's spinach on it.

There are seven minutes left of class when the loud-speaker beeps on. *"The election results are in!"* says the school secretary, and the room bursts into chatter. *"Remember to congratulate all the candidates who ran this year. Our new treasurer will be Max Hutchinson."* Max is in my class, so everyone cheers and people give him high fives.

"Our secretary will be Julia Miles." She's not in our class, so there's not much of a reaction.

"Our vice president is Zelda Martinez."

All my picks are winning so far. I'm three for three.

"And our student body president will be . . ."

I hold my breath.

"Zane Peterson!"

Some people cheer. Others moan. Despite my makeup tutorial, Brielle still has her supporters. Turns out, they're just not the majority.

Could it be my fault she lost? I mean, could one little parody really make someone change their mind about voting for Brielle?

I can't think like this. If she lost, it's because people thought Zane would make a better leader.

But after watching the speeches, I don't know how anyone with half a brain could believe that.

The clock says it's five till. Time to see the principal. I just gotta get through this one little chat, and I'm free to go home. Zane and I will do the talent show tomorrow, it'll be a big hit, and everyone will forget about the makeup tutorial. I've never been so ready for the weekend in my entire life.

My palms are sweaty, so I wipe them on my jeans before walking into Principal Duncan's office. I've been here a couple of times before, most notably after the slip-and-slide incident, but I've never felt bad about what I did until today.

Principal Duncan's office is speckled with green plants

in little clay pots. Sun filters through the window blinds, making it feel hot and muggy.

After I sit, Principal Duncan straightens his blue-striped tie. His frown looks more troubled than usual, the creases between his eyebrows extra deep. "I wanted to discuss a certain video that has been circulating through the school. I've been told it's disrupting class time."

So this *is* about the video. I wasn't paranoid after all.

I stare at the dying plant on his windowsill. "Did Brielle tell you?"

"Actually, it was Mr. Busby."

My ears burn. Mr. Busby is—*was*—one of the only teachers at this school who seemed to truly like me. Now he thinks I'm a jerk.

"Word is this video was meant to mock one of our students. Is that true?"

We both know who he's talking about. I might as well come out and say it.

I shrug and refuse to meet his eyes. "I guess it was kind of like Brielle's videos. We were just trying to be funny. It wasn't supposed to be mean."

I wish that were the truth so badly that it almost feels like it is.

Principal Duncan folds his hands over the desk. "I talked to Brielle briefly about the video to make sure she was okay. She said she was fine, but I could tell it really hurt her. As far as I'm concerned, this was online harassment. How would you feel if someone circulated a video making fun of you?"

I try to imagine it: someone, maybe Zane or Jared, re-creating my videos with a ridiculous-sounding voice. I can't believe it, but my throat starts to swell up. That's the world Brielle's living in right now, and it's because of me. I quickly wipe a hot tear from the corner of my eye, hoping Principal Duncan doesn't notice.

But he does. He hunches his shoulders, and his voice softens a little. "What's going through your mind, Jack?"

For the first time this whole conversation, I meet his eyes. "I didn't mean for this to be a big deal. It was supposed to be a joke."

"Some jokes are better left unsaid. You need to think of the real-life consequences your words can have on people. Especially when you're posting online."

"I wish I could take it back."

"That would be nice. But the internet is forever." He sighs. "Because the video was recorded off school grounds, this is under the jurisdiction of your parents. I called your mom to let her know, and she requested that you serve a week of after-school detention. We're running short on staff, so I talked her down to three days." He smiles a little. Maybe he doesn't hate me as much as I thought. Did he really have to tell Mom, though? She's going to be so disappointed. I worked hard to convince her I deserved my phone back. What if she takes it again?

Maybe it doesn't matter anymore.

"She said you could start after school today," Principal Duncan says.

Being free for the weekend has to wait after all. "Okay."

"Also, Mr. Busby has a couple of articles about online behavior and cyberbullying he'd like to share with you. He thinks you're a great kid, you know. We're hoping you can turn this into a learning opportunity."

One of the words he used pokes at me like a toothpick. "I never thought of myself as a bully."

"Well, you're not. But you did engage in bullying behavior. I trust you'll never do it again." He unfolds his hands. "Now, who else was in the video with you? The person behind your back?"

I want to tell the truth, but something won't let me. If I rat out Zane, our friendship is over. He's the only person I have left at this point.

I blink. "Some kid from another school."

Principal Duncan looks like he knows I'm lying. "Telling on a friend isn't snitching, you know. It's helping us reach that person so that maybe they can change their behavior."

What he's saying makes sense, but I stay silent. He can "reach" Zane through someone else. Lots of people must know by now he was the other guy in the video. I'm not gonna be the one to throw the new student body president under the bus.

The bell rings, and Principal Duncan says I'm free to go.

"Hey," I say, standing. "Thanks for the talk. And . . ." I wince. "Don't tell anyone I cried, okay?"

"I won't, but it's nothing to be embarrassed about. It's a sign of maturity to feel responsibility for your actions."

A sign of maturity. It's funny how the first time I've been called mature is right after crying. Maybe he's right, but I sure don't *feel* grown up.

"I just wish I could fix all this," I say.

"I'm sure you'll figure something out. You're clearly a very creative kid."

It's nice to be complimented on something other than being funny. I smile a little, even though I still feel like pond scum. "Thanks. I'll try."

21

A Sticky Situation

When I exit the principal's office, Zane's waiting down the hall, leaning against a classroom window. He jogs up to me. "Hey, I heard you got sent to the principal's. Like, three different people texted me. What happened? Was it about the video?"

His wide eyes tell me that he's as nervous as I was.

I put my hands into my pockets. "Yeah. He wanted to talk about how it was mean. Stuff like that."

"Did you tell him I was in it too?"

"Of course not."

"Oh, good!" He slaps my hand. "I only told a couple of people I was your arms. If Principal Duncan found out, it might make being the new president kind of awkward, you know?"

Zane might have been nervous, but he definitely doesn't feel guilty. Doesn't he realize how much damage we've done to Brielle?

Damage he benefited from, I guess. Mr. Student Body President.

"Anyway, now that I help plan the assemblies, next year we can come up with super-cool events." His face lights up. "Oh! What if we did a dance-off and got everyone to do the Toilet? We could record, like, an entire bleacherful of people doing it."

Normally, I'd be way into that, but something about My-Tube has left a sour taste in my mouth. It's like when I ate so many Cheetos that I threw up and never wanted them again.

Also, I'm 99 percent sure that Zane would dump me like a bag of trash the second I quit MyTube. Suddenly I don't feel like hanging out with him anymore.

"You're being quiet." Zane gives me a suspicious look.

"Yeah. I guess I'm still thinking about my talk with the principal. And about how I have to go to detention right now."

"Ah. That stinks. Guess I'll come over later tonight to practice for the show, then."

That's it? No *Too bad you have detention!* or *Sorry my dumb idea landed you there.* He doesn't feel bad about our video at all. Why am I not surprised?

"About the talent show . . ." I trail off. How can I break this to him without causing him to freak out? "I don't think I can do it anymore."

He draws his eyebrows together. "Why not?"

"I don't know. I'm just not feeling it."

Zane shakes his head and scoffs at the ceiling. "You're the one who thought it would be so epic."

"Well . . . I changed my mind." That's basically the truth. As much of it as he would understand, anyway.

"Whatever. You're acting really weird, you know?" He walks down the hall toward the door. "If you change your mind, don't bother asking me again."

Trust me, Zane, I think. This time, I won't.

Kids who get after-school detention are supposed to meet up in the cafeteria to get assigned to their service station. Basically, the gist of Franklin Middle School's philosophy is, "Let's ignore child labor laws by hiring fewer janitors and putting the bad kids to work." They tell us we're doing "service" to make us feel nice and fluffy inside, but it's hard to feel nice and fluffy when you're wiping down a toilet with one hand and plugging your nose with the other. I heard they're not allowed to assign bathroom cleaning anymore because of parental complaints. Those didn't come from my mom; that's for sure. She thinks I need to clean even *more* toilets. To be honest, I'd clean a hundred toilets if I could win back the election for Brielle.

I open the cafeteria door. What treasure awaits me today?

Inside, my social studies teacher, Mr. Felton, paces the floor like a prison warden. He oversees five or so students crouching under the lunch tables. "Keep working!" he barks to one kid who dares lie down on his watch. Looks like we're on gum-scraping duty today. Better than toilets, at least.

I quietly take my gum scraper and bag from Mr. Felton and head to a table that no one else is working on—the Table of Shame. Half a dozen wads of gum speckle its plastic belly, some fresh and gooey, others stale and gray. The blue wad of gum is the one that I put here when I was serving lunch detention a couple of weeks ago.

There's a wall in Seattle—some sort of tourist attraction—that's covered inches thick with chewed gum. I've seen people on MyTube posing in front of it and smiling. The photos probably do no justice to how disgusting that wall is in real life. Pictures never show the full story.

I pick at a gooey wad using the trash bag as a makeshift glove. It has a chunk of tortilla chip in it, and I gag. In my old days, I would have recorded me pretending to eat that chip, but I don't even feel like it now.

Mr. Felton brings in some gloves and a bucket of soapy water so we can wipe the tabletops. I scrape at a stubborn wad and check the clock. It's only been six minutes, and we're here for thirty. Beneath the clock, the gray kitten stares at me from its poster. "Hang in there!" it says, clinging to its branch.

"Hey," the guy at the next table whispers at me. He's the one who was trying to lie down earlier. "What are you and Zane doing for the talent show tomorrow?"

I stick another gum wad into my trash bag. "We're not doing it anymore."

"Why? Zane said you guys had something planned."

How many times am I gonna get asked about this? I don't even have a good answer. "We did, but some stuff came up."

"Ah. Oh well."

He sure doesn't seem torn up about it. Maybe people care less about my act than I thought. I mean, the whole two weeks I didn't have my account, not one person said they missed it. No one's world exploded because I wasn't constantly updating them on the details of my life. It all feels so fake. Maybe I should delete MyTube altogether.

I don't know if I could go that far. But there's something I could start with. . . .

When Mr. Felton turns his back, I pull up the makeup tutorial and press Delete. A surge of relief rushes through me. I don't care what Zane will say. I'm just glad it's gone.

Next I need to apologize to Brielle. In person. Mr. Busby would say that's the only way to show her I mean it. As much as I don't want to get yelled at again, I need to get this off my chest before it crushes me to a pulp. I wonder if she's at speed friendshipping right now. She mentioned it in her speech. Maybe it's worth dropping by to find out.

I need to get out of here. Luckily, I have mastered the art of escape.

I walk over to Mr. Felton and twist up my face. "I really need to go to the bathroom."

Teachers don't usually believe me when I use this excuse, because 90 percent of the time, it's not true. But I've discovered that if I look miserable enough, I can plant a sliver of doubt in their mind, and that sliver will eat away at their conscience until they agree to let me go.

Mr. Felton crosses his arms. "Not buying it." He's always been a tough egg to crack.

I moan. "But I *really* have to go."

Then, as if on cue, my stomach grumbles. Bless the gods of stomach juices!

Mr. Felton winces, and I can almost hear his shell cracking. He probably thinks the hunger groan was more of an I-need-to-use-the-bathroom groan, which is embarrassing, but if it works in my favor, I'll go with it. I clutch my stomach and mouth, *"Please."*

He grunts. "Fine. But no dillydallying. I mean it."

I salute him and head out the door. Considering he thinks I have stomach issues, I figure I have about ten minutes before I have to come back. Better make them good.

22

The Last Speed Friendshipping

I jog to the drama room and sneak in. Several people turn to look as I stand awkwardly by the door. I wonder what they're thinking. Most of the kids who go to speed friendshipping are, as you would expect, "good kids." I feel like I'm no longer welcome here, despite the phrase "You belong here" that's still scribbled on the whiteboard from the first meeting.

I'm not sure how to enter the conversations now that they've already started. Mario's paired up with Tasha, but there's no sign of Brielle. I nod at Tasha, and she nods back. I asked her before math if she heard back from that fashion contest. Turns out she lost. She said the winner had thousands of followers and she never had a chance. I bet she'd have had a shot if it weren't for me.

Mr. Busby catches my eye and gives me a confused look. I wonder if he knows I'm supposed to be in detention right now.

I almost turn right around, since Brielle's not here anyway, but Mr. Busby waves me over to his spot by the whiteboard. I force my feet to walk over. I can't run away or he might tell the principal on me.

"Glad you made it." He dings the bell, and the people in the green chairs shift. Mr. Busby adds a chair to the end of each aisle and sits in one of them. "You can start by being my partner."

Great. He probably wants to give some spiel about cyberbullying or whatever. I am so done talking about this! I sit down anyway and brace myself for the lecture.

Mr. Busby places his hands on his lap and looks me straight in the eye. He's really into the whole eye-contact thing, but I can never decide if it makes me feel understood or just plain uncomfortable.

"Since this is our last speed friendshipping, we're discussing what we want to keep and what we want to change when we start up again next year."

I'm surprised at how sad I feel. "Why is this the last speed friendshipping?"

"Next Friday, the teachers have a meeting after school.

The Friday after that is the last day of school. So, what have you enjoyed about your experiences here?"

I almost say, "The doughnuts," but I want to be real with him. He's always real with us. "Everyone here is really nice. No one cares who your friends are or what group you belong to. Lots of these people I never would've talked to if it weren't for this. Some of us even hung out."

"Oh yeah? Who?"

I stare at my hands. "Mario, Tasha, and Brielle." What stinks is that every one of them is worse off because of me. Mario wouldn't have gotten grounded. Tasha could have won her fashion contest. Brielle could have been our student body president.

"That's great!" says Mr. Busby.

"Not really," I mumble without meaning to.

"Why do you say that?"

I sigh and kick my toe against the ground. "I don't know. I wasn't a great friend. It probably would've been better if they never met me in the first place."

Mr. Busby nods slowly. "Life would be easier if we never had to deal with people. But it would also be pretty boring, wouldn't it?"

"I guess." Hanging out with Mario, Brielle, and Tasha led to some of the funnest times I've had all year. Even more fun than T-rexing through JOANN's.

"You'll always make mistakes in a friendship," Mr. Busby says. "The question is how you make up for them."

"Some things you can't fix."

"Maybe not. But it's worth trying."

So far, I haven't tried making anything up to anyone. I thought the best thing was to leave people alone so they didn't have to deal with me anymore. But that was a cop-out.

When Tasha taught me how to push through the hard problems in math, I ended up with the highest test score I've ever gotten in my life.

Maybe it's the same with friends.

I look at Mario and an idea starts brewing. He's two seats down on the opposite side. At two minutes a conversation, I could talk with him and still make it back to detention within my ten-minute window.

Mr. Busby dings the bell, and I shoot Brielle a text while I'm shifting seats: "Can we talk?" A few seconds later, the message is marked as "read." I wonder how long it will take her to answer, if she even does.

My next turn is with Michael Lee, and then Mei-ling. We talk about ideas we have for speed friendshipping next year. Michael wants a day where we play our favorite songs. Mei-ling wants to have group games during the first ten minutes. Then we talk about our summer plans and exchange numbers. My aunt has a pool. Maybe she'll let me have a swim party this summer and invite everyone.

Finally I take the seat in front of Mario. "Hey."

His mouth forms that pressed-lip smile you make when you pass a stranger in the hall. I wonder if he knows about the makeup tutorial, since he doesn't have MyTube. It must be nice to not deal with any of that drama.

There's a silence between us that feels like my fault. "We haven't hung out in a while," I finally say. Way to state the obvious.

Mario shrugs. "I didn't think you wanted to."

"I didn't think you wanted to either."

"I never acted mad, did I?"

"Not really," I say. "Did I act mad?"

"Well, no. But it seemed like you ditched me because I couldn't do the talent show anymore."

The truth is, that was part of it. *You use people when it benefits you*, Brielle said. She was right.

"I'm sorry," I say. "It might have been that way at first. But I really do want to hang out again."

He nods. "I'd be cool with that."

"Speaking of the talent show . . . Do you think you could make me a decent hacky sack player by tomorrow?"

Mario looks confused. "What about the food dartboard?"

"I think it'd be cooler if we did our hacky sack routine. What do you think?"

"Seriously? That would be sweet!" He bites his bottom lip. "Are you sure, though? It wouldn't make a very good MyTube video."

"I don't care about that anymore." And it's true. I couldn't care less about recording our act. It'll be fun either way.

Mario and I make plans to meet at his house one hour before the show to practice. I try to convince him to get those fire hacky sacks he was telling me about. He says he doesn't want to get grounded again, so I don't push it.

Making up with Mario was fairly easy. Making up with Brielle? That could be brutal. I read over my message to her: "Can we talk?" Still no answer.

As I walk back to detention, my phone dings. Brielle sent a one-word reply. "Sure."

23

Three Compliments

I ask Brielle for her address, and after detention, Mom drops me off in front of her house. Brielle lives in a neighborhood close to mine, so I can walk home when I'm done. At first, Mom didn't think I deserved to go to a friend's, but when I explained who Brielle was and how I wanted to apologize in person, Mom agreed. "That's very mature of you," she said, making it the second time I've been called that. A strange day, indeed.

Brielle's house reminds me of a fancy version of a fairy-tale cottage. White window shutters hang over a little flower garden, and the bright green grass is perfectly trimmed.

I freeze at the door. For all I know, Brielle's just letting me come over so she can chew me out or throw something in my face. Like pie. Or spaghetti, since we all know that's the best food to throw when you're mad.

I ring the doorbell anyway and hold my breath as it echoes inside.

The door opens slowly. It's Brielle, with no spaghetti in hand. She crosses her arms over her sweatshirt. "What did you want to talk about, Jack?"

I shuffle my feet and stare at the cursive *W* on the welcome mat. "I, uh, just wanted to see if you had any pizza left over. That spinach kind you posted about yesterday looked pretty tasty."

She glares at me. "If you came over here to make fun of me, you can leave."

"No! I'm sorry. I'm sorry." I wring my hands. "I guess I just make jokes when I don't know what to say."

"Why'd you come if you didn't know what to say?"

I don't answer quickly enough, so she starts to shut the door.

"Wait!"

She pauses and stares expectantly. This is going terribly. No more jokes.

"I should never have posted that video. It was mean and stupid and extremely uncool. I know that doesn't fix what happened to you. I'd do anything to take it back. I'd delete my account entirely. Or eat a cockroach."

"That's not saying much." Her arms are still crossed. "You'd eat a cockroach just to make people laugh."

"Good point. I don't expect you to forgive me. I just wanted to let you know how sorry I am. And I wanted to give you this." I dig into my back pocket and hold up a colorful paper bracelet.

She eyes it suspiciously. "What's this?"

"Well . . ." I twist the bracelet lightly around my fingers. "You know how you won the last time we played table football? And I offered you my Starbursts, but you didn't want them because of your no-sugar thing? Well, I started making you a bracelet out of the wrappers that night. I know it's not fashionable, but I thought you'd think it was funny. Then we got in that fight and I never gave it to you, but I figured, I can't just throw it away. I mean, *you* can throw it away if you want, but I thought you might as well see it for, like . . . old times' sake, I guess?" I pause and scratch my arm. I really don't know where I'm going with this.

Brielle holds out her hand, and I drop the bracelet into her palm. "I like it." She tucks it carefully into the pocket of her jeans and motions to the steel bench on the porch. "Wanna sit?"

We move to the bench. I take one of the red throw pillows and put it on my lap. Brielle sits next to me and hunches her shoulders. "Your video made me look really shallow, you know? That's exactly what I've been trying to avoid."

A sad look clouds over her eyes, and I can see that what I did was worse than the jerks making rude comments on her posts. I knew she wanted people to see her differently, but I made the video anyway. Brielle's not just the smiley, confident girl from her makeup tutorials. She worries about what people think, same as everyone else.

I lower my head. "I'm so sorry, Brielle. I know it's my fault you lost the election. You totally deserved to win."

"Go on," she says with an unreadable expression.

"I mean, you were clearly the better choice. You care about the school. You always follow through. And most of all, you are *not* shallow."

She crosses her legs on the bench. "Do you remember the first time we talked?"

"Didn't I say something to you in fifth grade about burping or something?"

"What?" she snorts. "I'm talking about at speed friend-shipping."

"Oh." I try to remember. "We had to give each other compliments, right?"

"Yeah. Do you remember what your compliments were?"

I shake my head.

"You said you liked my hair and my clothes. That's all people ever notice about me. Maybe it's my fault. I'm always trying to make people think my life is perfect, when it's obviously not."

We sit in silence for a while as birds whistle from the tree above us. I wipe dust off the bench's arm with my finger, deep in thought. "Can I have a do-over?"

She looks at me. "Huh?"

"I know you better now. I could come up with different compliments."

She purses her lips. "Well . . . okay."

I hold up a finger. "Compliment number one: you are the hardest worker I know. I think it's cool that you join clubs and volunteer and stuff. And even though I made fun of it, I'm actually really impressed with your makeup skills. That stuff is not easy to put on."

She laughs. "You think?"

"Compliment number two: you're fun to be around. Clothespinning at the mall was probably the best time I've ever had making a video."

"Yeah, that was awesome." Her eyes don't look sad anymore, and I can tell she's enjoying being complimented.

"And three?" she asks.

"Well, you're talking to me right now. I always try to avoid people when I'm mad at them. The fact that you let me come over says a lot about you."

"I guess it's cool you came to talk to me too. Those things I said to you in the hall . . ." She tugs at her sleeve. "I feel really bad about that."

"It's already forgotten." I study her face. "Are you gonna be okay?"

"I'm just glad it's almost summer. I'm out of friends for the moment, so I'm not looking forward to lunch for the next week."

"Trust me, I know how you feel. What happened with your friends?"

Brielle brings her knees up and hugs them in front of her. "In the bathroom after school, I overheard Devyn talking to Shawna. Devyn was glad I lost the election. She was all, 'Brielle gets everything she wants. It's about time she lost something.' Shawna agreed, and they both laughed."

"They don't sound like good friends."

"They're not." Her voice cracks. "I've known it for a while. But Devyn and I have been friends since, like, fourth grade, and I don't have anyone else."

"Some friends are worth fighting for, and some are worth letting go of." That line sounded straight out of a fortune cookie. Mr. Busby must be rubbing off on me.

"Take Zane and me, for example," I continue. "We're history. And I feel surprisingly good about it. Friends should make you feel better about yourself, not worse. The good thing is that there are lots of other people who would want to be friends with you."

"Yeah, maybe you're right." Her eyes lighten a bit, and she goes back to sitting cross-legged on the bench. "So, if you're not hanging out with Zane anymore, does that mean you're not doing the talent show? I heard it was back on with you two."

"Mario and I are gonna hacky-sack instead."

"That'll be fun to watch."

"Yeah." I bump her shoulder. "We might even be better than your dancing."

"Don't worry about competition from me. I'm quitting the show. I was planning to email Ms. Campbell about taking me off the list."

"What? But you're so good. You *have* to perform."

She shakes her head. "I never wanted to in the first place. I only signed up because my mom pressured me to. Dancing doesn't feel fun anymore. I'm taking a break for now." I can tell she's made up her mind.

A sly smile creeps onto her face. "Besides, I need to free up time to make room for . . . other responsibilities."

"What's with the face? What's going on?"

She bites her lip and shrugs, but I nudge her a couple of times. "Spill."

"Okay, okay. I did get one piece of good news today. Principal Duncan called after school. Turns out the ballot box was stuffed with fake votes for Zane. He got disqualified, so I'm officially president."

My jaw drops. "You're kidding! That's amazing!"

"I know! I was shocked when I got the phone call. I was so sure I'd lost in a landslide."

"Wait. So I *didn't* lose the election for you, then."

"Nope." She smirks. "But it was fun watching you squirm."

It makes total sense. How could Zane win when he's not even nice to anyone? Brielle's the one who tried to get to know new people. A mean video couldn't erase that. I couldn't have lost the election for her if I'd tried.

"Well, what should we do to celebrate?" I grab her shoulders. "This is huge!"

"We could do that stupid happy dance you always do." She mimics the way I bop my head to the left and right. "Uh-huh. Uh-huh."

"Hey, you're doing the head bop all wrong. You gotta keep your chin level."

"Oh, I'm sorry. Did I mess up the head bop? How could I possibly?"

After I correct her form, Brielle and I improvise some new moves to add to the dance so it's not so "monotonous" (her word, not mine). She frames her face with her hands. "Too bad the talent show audience won't see this."

"About the talent show . . . you haven't emailed Ms. Campbell about quitting yet, have you?"

"No. Why? I was kidding about doing the happy dance, you know."

"Yeah, but you're good at lots of stuff. Maybe instead of dancing, you could do something else."

"Like what? It's not like I can teach everyone how to apply blush or how to pair a scarf with their shoes."

Wait a second . . . how to pair a scarf . . . "That's it!" I hop off the bench and punch my arms in the air repeatedly.

"What in the world are you talking about?"

I drop my arms. "You're gonna love this. But we've got a lot of work to do."

24

Taking Turns

Brielle and I spend two hours Saturday morning preparing her slot for the talent show. As the idea evolves, we realize we're gonna need backup. I text Mario and Axel, and Brielle texts Mei-ling. One by one, they show up at my house and we give them their assignments. Jacob pops in near the end and watches our run-though. He claps loudly and gives me a fist bump. I hope things go over as well with the audience. This is the type of act that'll either be epically entertaining, or a cringey flop. We'll find out which soon enough.

At six o'clock, my entire family and I drive to the school. I don't remember the last time we all went to something together. Josh gave up going to a birthday party to be here,

249

and Jacob gave up studying for a test. Josh even agreed to be my cameraman for Brielle's slot. He wants to add some pre- and post-narration. That kid loves the camera even more than I do.

I meet up with Mario, and we check in backstage by writing our names on a clipboard. Ms. Campbell tells us to wait in the orchestra room until we're called to perform. In the room, stacked chairs are pushed against the walls, and everyone's practicing their acts. Some run through chore- ography in brightly colored costumes, and others sing vo- cal warm-ups. The double Dutchers have claimed the center of the room, and several instruments play over each other, mixing together like musical soup. Brielle, Axel, and Mei- ling huddle in the corner to chat, and Mario and I kick a hacky sack around. I grab Brielle and teach her how to bounce it off her knee, but she accidentally hits it onto the side of some dude's cello. Luckily, there's no damage.

About thirty minutes in, Mario and I are called for our turn. I stuff the hacky sack into my pocket, and we wait backstage.

"Are you nervous?" Mario rubs his hands together like he's lighting a fire.

"Nah. Everyone will love this."

"I've never performed onstage before," Mario says. He runs his hands through his hair three times.

"Dude. You're gonna have super-poofy hair if you keep doing that. Just take some deep breaths, in and out."

He gulps down a few breaths and heaves them back out. It doesn't look as classy as when Brielle does it, but hopefully it works just as well.

The act before us ends, and the auditorium fills with applause. The emcee lady's voice rings out in the microphone. "Wonderful! Thank you for sharing your talent. I've never seen anyone pogo so high! Next up, we have Mario Hernandez and Jack Reynolds, ready to thrill us with a hacky sack routine. Good luck, boys!"

We jog onto the stage, and the crowd cheers as the *Pokémon* theme song blares in the background. That was Mario's idea, since it was such a hit during my audition.

Mario tosses me the hacky sack and lets me start. I do a couple of simple kicks, but I drop the sack on my third try. I pretend it was on purpose by somersaulting and grabbing it midroll. Then I throw it like a Poké Ball to Mario.

Mario starts with one of his hardest tricks: the Rainbow Kick. He turns to the side and kicks the hacky sack above his head, so it travels over him like a rainbow. Then he bends his foot back and kicks it over his head in the opposite direction, the rainbow traveling back. The crowd goes wild.

We take turns passing the sack back and forth. Mario's turns take a little longer since he actually knows what he's doing. He spins while the sack is in the air and kicks to the beat of the song. During another turn, he stalls the sack on the back of his neck before flinging it up and catching it on his knee.

I stick to more simple tricks. I tiptoe around while balancing the sack on my nose like a seal. For the grand finale, I wrap a piece of masking tape around the hacky sack and lasso it above my head. Between Mario's skill and my comedy, we make a good team.

The music stops, and we take a bow. I bow so low that it morphs into one final somersault, complete with a pose. I scan the audience and spot Mom, Dad, Josh, and Jacob standing and cheering at the top of their lungs. I take a mental picture: the bright lights, the smiling audience, the feeling of Mario slapping my back and my family up on their feet. These are the things you can't capture with a camera.

Ms. Campbell meets us backstage and high-fives us. "Well done! You guys are natural performers." She checks her clipboard. "There's one act to go, and then your speed-friendshipping group is up."

Mario and I rush to the orchestra room to grab everyone. I hope Tasha took my advice and got a good seat. I want her to be close enough that I can see the shocked look on her face.

Tasha's the type of person who never shows off, even though she's super talented. Brielle and I figured it's about time someone else showed off for her.

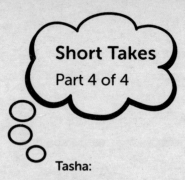

Tasha

Tasha:

The pianist hits the last note of "Flight of the Bumble-bee" with a flourish of her hand, and the audience erupts with applause. I've never seen anyone's fingers move that fast! I swear they looked blurry.

Mom opens her program and leans close to me. "Looks like your friend Brielle's up next." It's funny how Mom thinks Brielle and I are friends just because I went to her house once. I don't correct her, though. It's partially my fault that I'm not better friends with Brielle. She hasn't been talking to me, but I haven't tried either.

This week, something clicked. Jack came to talk to me at lunch on Monday, and when he mentioned my designs, everyone at my table acted clueless. It was so embarrassing that my "best friends" didn't know about my biggest hobby. Jack probably knew right then and there I was a loner who just tagged along. But after he left, Kayla started telling me about how she's into cross-stitch, and I realized I didn't know anything about her. And why would I? I never asked.

It's like Mr. Busby says: _There's nothing more inter-_

esting than people. Once I started asking the girls more questions, lunch has gotten a lot more fun. I wouldn't even mind coming back to Franklin next year. I told Mom our new house should be in the school district. She said she we could try, but no promises.

The girl onstage bows, and the bumblebee antennas attached to her head boing all over. I'm glad Jack convinced me to come tonight. I would've hated to miss the hacky sack routine. Jack was hilarious, and Mario was jaw-droppingly amazing. (Oh, Mario. There are no words.) Plus, it's been nice to get out with Mom. Now that renovations are almost done, I'm hoping we can do stuff like this more often.

Mom and I have been talking more lately. I think it started after DeAndre's birthday celebration. Mom helped me fill the living room with orange streamers and orange balloons—DeAndre's favorite color. Dad came over, and we watched the slideshow I made on Mom's laptop. I had collected all the photos I could find of our family the way it used to be: Mom, Dad, DeAndre, and me, happy, smiling, and together.

It was a night I'll always remember. We cried, we laughed, we talked about our favorite DeAndre moments, and we ate cake. We felt like a family again. When Dad left, Mom even hugged him goodbye. I know it's not smart to get my hopes up, but I can't help it. A little hope fluttered in my heart, and I can't bring myself to squash it. I'll let it stay as long as it wants.

"Can I sit here?" a deep voice says from the aisle.

I gasp. "Dad!" I leap into the aisle and wrap my arms around his waist. When I look back at Mom, she's smiling knowingly. She must have invited him. The hope in my chest flutters harder.

"I heard tonight was going to be pretty special." Dad winks at Mom. What in the world? Mom scoots down a seat and motions for me to do the same. I do, and watch Dad's face to check if he winks again.

The bumblebee girl walks offstage, and Brielle takes the mic. "Hello, everyone." Her voice sounds a little shaky. "Your programs say I'm dancing tonight, but my friends and I, with the permission of the directors, have changed my act to something even better."

I notice her outfit, and my mouth falls open. It's my dress! The one I was going to submit to the fashion contest. It looks great on her. You can't even tell it was ever stained, thanks to the stain-remover recipe I found online.

I look at Mom. "Is that . . . ? But how?"

She puts her arm around me. "Jack and Brielle came over this morning while you were babysitting. They wanted to model your designs, so I let them borrow some outfits. Since you weren't home, they decided to make it a surprise."

My voice gets caught in my throat. This might be the nicest thing anyone's ever done for me.

Brielle sweeps her arms toward the stage. "Introducing the fashion designs of Tasha Moore."

Runway music starts to play, and the singer shouts, "You better work!" Mei-ling is first up. She struts from one side of the stage to the other, stopping in the middle to pose. It's a surreal experience—almost like I'm living out my favorite daydream, where I'm at New York Fashion Week, watching the models strut down the runway in my designs.

Brielle reads from a slip of paper. "Mei-ling is wearing a dusty rose chiffon skirt, each layer sewn on by Tasha herself. This pairs beautifully with a cream V-neck. Perfect for any occasion!"

"That's beautiful," Mom says. "You should make it in my size."

Jack swaggers out next, and everyone laughs. He's wearing, like, ten of my hats at once: two on his head, two as gloves, and several pinned to his shirt.

"Why wear one hat when you can wear them all?" Brielle says. "Each of these original creations has its own unique style and color. Whether you're looking for a snug beanie or a summer hat, a zigzag pattern or a flower embellishment, Tasha can crochet whatever style you like." Jack makes a show of putting different hats on his head, and then does a floppy cartwheel off the stage.

Axel comes out next, wearing sunglasses and a trench coat. I cover my mouth and giggle. He's the last person I would expect to participate in a fashion show. He's wearing the skull beanie he paid me to crochet him last week.

"Here we have Axel sporting a knitted black scarf and a hat with a skull on it," Brielle says. "A perfect look for the artistic, broody type." Axel shuffles across the stage, spinning on his heels once he reaches the middle. He points to the skull and bops his head.

Mario steps onstage next, and my heart leaps into my throat. He's wearing the gray blazer I designed for DeAndre. It fits him perfectly.

"This cotton blazer has been hemmed, fitted, and embellished with bright orange pockets and buttons," Brielle says. "Quirky and stylish, this outfit is sure to be a conversation starter. Pair it with jeans for formal occasions, or with shorts for a more relaxed look."

After Mario goes offstage, Jack takes the microphone from Brielle and asks her to spin.

"Last, let's all admire Brielle's outfit," he says. "It's inspired by the 1920s flapping dresses."

"*Flapper* dresses," Brielle corrects him.

"Right," says Jack. "My favorite part is the pom-poms at the bottom. Especially how they look when you spin. Spin faster, Brielle. Throw in a dance move!"

Brielle twirls in a pirouette, and the pom-poms flare out.

She laughs and takes the mic back. "Give it up one last time for the best seventh-grade designer in all of Utah, Tasha Moore."

Jack steals the mic. "Stand up, Tasha!"

Mom nudges me. "Go on."

My knees feel shaky, but I stand and wave. I feel bright and warm, almost as if the spotlights above the stage are shining right through me. Some people in the audience get on their feet and cheer, and I swallow hard to hold back tears. It'd be so embarrassing to cry in front of everyone. When I sit back down, Mom squeezes my knee, and Dad leans in to kiss the side of my head. "I'm so proud of you," he says, and my heart swells up like a balloon. I wish DeAndre were here to be proud of me too. But I have a feeling that some-how, even though I can't see him, he is.

Mario:

My heart was pounding so hard throughout our hacky sack rou-tine. I probably would have got-ten a heart attack and fallen offstage if it hadn't been for Jack. During each of his turns, I was able to calm down and laugh a little. He's lucky he doesn't get stage fright.

Mario

Mom and Dad say I didn't look nervous, but they have to say that because I'm their son. They also didn't notice that I dropped the sack right after I stalled it on my neck. I kicked it back up pretty fast, so it might have looked intentional.

As much fun as it was to show off my hacky sack skills, I liked the fashion show even more. For one, all I had to do was walk down the stage, which was easy. But the best part was seeing Tasha's face. I've never seen her smile so big.

Perry was supposed to come, but I didn't see him. I bet he was home gaming with Phineas. They're, like, best friends now. I don't mind, especially since Jack is down to hang out again. He and I are planning a pool party on the first day of summer vacation for all the people who went to speed friendshipping. We'll still invite Perry and Phineas, but I doubt they'll come.

After our fashion show, we went back to the orchestra room, and Brielle collected our clothes to return to Tasha. That blazer was way cool. It's not really my style, but I might ask Tasha if I could pay her to make me one for special occasions. I was bummed I didn't have time to talk to her after the show. Mom and Dad rushed me home because it was past the twins' bedtime.

On Sunday morning, my parents call me to the kitchen table and say they want to talk. I squeak back a chair and sit, wondering what this could be about.

"We've been thinking about the slideshow you showed us last week," Mom says.

I gulp. Did it work? Are they getting me a phone?

"Don't get too excited," Dad says, like he's reading my mind. He pulls a slim, black phone out of his pocket and hands it to me. "This is not a smartphone."

I swipe my thumb across the touchscreen, too confused to be excited. It looks like a smartphone. It feels like a smartphone. Is this some weird metaphor?

"This is a Gabb Wireless phone," Dad says. "The world's dumbest smartphone. No internet. No apps. No games. But it does text and make calls."

I turn it over in my hand. At least it looks cool. It's a major step up from having nothing. "It's mine?" I ask, just to make sure.

"It is," Mom says. "We understand you want to be able to communicate better with your friends. From what we saw last night, it looks like you have some great ones."

"Thanks for the phone." I get up and hug them both. A "dumbphone" isn't exactly what I asked for, but at least I know they were listening and are willing to meet me halfway. Or at least, like, an eighth of the way.

"Can I borrow your phone to copy down some numbers?" I ask Mom.

She hands it over. "Sure." I save Jack as a contact.

"Now, don't overdo anything," Mom says. "We don't want you texting for hours on end."

"I won't." That sounds boring anyway. I don't want to be like Perry, constantly sending platypus GIFs.

My first message is to Jack: *Hey dude. Guess who can text now?*

Jack: *Is this Mario? No way! Your parents finally caved?*

Me: *Kind of. This phone only texts. No MyTube or anything like that.*

Jack: *Honestly, that's probably better.*

Me: *Hey, do you have Tasha's number? I didn't get to congratulate her last night.*

Jack: *Yeah. One sec . . .*

Now I can tell her how much I liked that blazer.

Brielle:

There's a poster in the school cafeteria of a cat looking out a window. It says, "After the rain comes
the rainbow." If that's true, then
Friday was the rain, and Saturday
was the rainbow. On Friday, I felt
like everyone hated me and I'd
never have friends again. But on

Saturday, I realized I have more friends than
ever before. My speed-friendshipping people have my
back. I told Mei-ling about the Devyn drama, and she
said I could sit with her and her friends at lunch. I don't
know why I never asked to before.

After the show, I found Tasha in the audience and
handed back her bag of clothes. "Your designs are
amazing. Thanks for letting us show them off." Then
I remembered she never okayed the idea. "I mean,
not like you had a choice. Sorry if we should have
asked."

She hugged me, which surprised me so much

263

that it took a second to remember to hug her back. "Thanks so much," she said. "This means more than you'll ever know."

"It was fun," I said. "By the way, I hope you weren't embarrassed having to stand at the end. That was all Jack. I told him not to do it, but he never listens."

"He really doesn't, right?" We both laughed. I'll have to have her over to make cookies again. I could invite Mei-ling too. I can see them getting along.

That night, Jack texted me a screenshot of a photo. "I was gonna post this on MyTube," he said, "but I wanted to check with you first."

I zoomed in to read the caption:

This girl. There's so much more than meets the eye. She's fun and kind, and she'll ROCK being student body president. One of the last people I thought would be my friend because she's way too cool for me. Thanks for putting up with me, Bri Bri ☺

I smiled and read it over again. Jack's determined to make me forget about the makeup tutorial. So far, it's been working.

Next I zoomed in on the photo. It was me in Tasha's white dress. He must have taken it in the orchestra room when I wasn't looking. I was midlaugh, standing across from Mei-ling with a cello in the background. The light hit my hair just right so my highlights stood

out, and my lipstick was perfect. Normally, I'd be ach-
ing to post a photo like this.

But why? I've been so concerned with impressing
my followers that I haven't been able to just enjoy the
good things that happen.

I texted back: "I love this, Jack, but don't worry
about posting it. It means more knowing you were
going to. Oh, and DON'T call me Bri Bri! 😊"

Not everyone had to know what Jack thought
of me. They wouldn't understand. Now I wouldn't
waste time following the reactions, or stressing over
rude comments from people who don't matter and
shouldn't be part of my life. It felt freeing, like washing
off heavy makeup after a long day.

I opened MyTube and tapped around until I found
what I was looking for. The message popped up on
the screen:

Are you sure you want to deactivate your account?

YES   NO

My thumb hovered over the choices. Would I re-
gret this? I've invested so much time and energy into
building my following and my image. It's been a part
of who I am for so long.

I pressed YES.

My image is not who I am. It never was.

25

The Raccoon Whisperer

It's hard to crouch in a dinosaur costume. It's even harder to hold your head up. You know how newborns have terrible neck control because their heads are too big for their bodies? T. rexes must have had the same problem.

"Any raccoons yet?" I ask Mario. I take off my dino head and set it in the dirt. Then I peek out from behind the bushes, squinting down the driveway. In the moonlight, I can't make out much. "Maybe we should call it quits. My neck hurts."

"No way! Keep your eye on the prize." Mario readjusts his bear ears. "Besides, you're the one who insisted on wearing the T. rex costume."

"At least I'm more terrifying than you, Mr. Fuzzy Wuzzy." He looks ridiculous in his woolly purple turtleneck and ears headband. We're supposed to look like natural predators to scare the raccoons off, but he looks more like one of the plushies from Build-A-Bear Workshop. According to him, raccoons are color-blind, so it doesn't matter if the sweater is purple as long as it's fuzzy.

Mario's mom let him come over for a late night, which is basically a sleepover without the "sleeping over" part. Dad offered us fifty bucks yesterday if we could find a way to keep the raccoons out of the trash bins for good, so we've spent the last two nights experimenting. I'm letting Mario call the shots tonight since my last attempt was a major fail. Turns out that when you spread honey on the sidewalk in front of the trash bins, the raccoons won't eat that *instead* of the trash. They'll eat that *and* the trash.

Plus, you'll get ants. Lots of ants.

"You really think this will work?" I give up on crouching and try to balance on my thick green tail.

"Yeah. It's called Pavlovian training. If the raccoons associate the trash bins with terror, they'll stop coming back."

"Taking your word for it, Dr. Mario."

Mario pulls his sleeve up and scratches his forearm. "Your mom's sweater is, like, full of ticks, I swear."

"It probably is. It's been lying in the outside shed for the past month."

"Dude!" He tosses a pine cone at my plushy stomach. "You'd better be kidding."

I throw up my hands. "I am! I am!"

The leaves of a nearby bush rustle, and I suck in my breath. "That's gotta be a raccoon!" I whisper, returning to crouching position. Squinting through the leaves, I make out a gray-and-black figure scurrying out of the bush. His feet pitter-patter across the sidewalk until they reach the trash bins. He backs up for a running start and then leaps onto the lid and starts prying it open. Little dude's got skills.

I grab my dino head off the ground and speak softly. "All right, on the count of three, we pop out and roar." I put on the head. "One . . . two . . ."

"Wait!" Mario grabs my shoulder. "It's kind of cute. Maybe this is mean."

"You can't turn back now! What about the fifty bucks?"

"Just look at him, Jack!"

The raccoon has pried the lid all the way open. His striped bushy tail swishes as he perches on the bin's edge. Beady eyes gleam inside his black furry mask, and he rubs his paws together like he's about to dig into a buffet.

"Okay, it's a little cute," I admit. "But this is for his own good. What if my dad ends up calling pest control?"

"True. But this might not be the best way to get rid of him. What if he attacks us?"

"No way!" I point at my head. "I'm a T. rex. I'm terrifying."

"You're not that terrifying."

I place my hand on my chest. "My roar would strike fear into the heart of any creature."

"Please. It couldn't scare a kitten."

"Oh yeah?" Sorry, raccoon, but Mario has questioned my roaring skills. "Watch this."

I hop out from behind the bush and wriggle my arms. "GRAWUUUREEEEAAAARRR!"

Through the thick dino head, I hear a loud hiss. That couldn't have been . . .

"Uh-oh." Mario's voice is shaky. "He's coming for you."

"Huh?"

"Run!"

My heart pounds along with my feet across the driveway. I tug off my dino head and toss it onto the front lawn. There aren't any cars, so I dart across the cul-de-sac, the raccoon chasing behind.

I run in wide circles, hoping to wear him down. When I veer

into Mr. Finley's lawn, I catch him peeping at me through his window blinds, so I quickly return to the sidewalk.

I think I'm safe now, but I scan my surroundings just to be sure. Five feet ahead of me, the raccoon creeps out of the rosebushes and freezes on the cement. We lock eyes. Both of us stand our ground like we're facing off in an old Western movie. I wouldn't be surprised if a tumbleweed rolled by.

I've got to get away before the situation escalates. I lift one foot and carefully slide it backward.

The raccoon hisses and bares his teeth. Gah!

The chase continues, and Mario calls directions from my driveway: "Turn right! Turn left!"

"Jack!" he shouts, extra alarmed. "He's on your tail!"

"I know!" I shout back.

"No, literally. On your *tail*!"

Then I get it. I hear rustling as the little devil scampers his way up my costume. What if he scratches my face and I get rabies? I'm too young to die!

I spin like a tornado, the view of my cul-de-sac becoming a grayish blur. The raccoon tumbles off my back and skitters into the neighbor's bushes.

"I think you lost him!" Mario shouts. I rest my hands on my knees and pant, waiting for my head to stop spinning.

Mario snorts. "Yeah, looks like your roar *really* scared that raccoon."

"That was no ordinary raccoon!" I shout as I head back. "That was some kind of fearless mutant!"

He laughs. "I can't wait to tell Tasha and Brielle about this."

"As long as you tell them how I totally kicked his butt!"

"Fine, deal." He kicks a pine cone as we walk up my driveway. "I bet he comes back, though. We need another plan. What should we try next?"

I rub my chin. "Maybe we can sprinkle gross food over the top of the trash. Like those fish sticks we burnt yesterday."

"Yeah, those were nasty. I bet even a raccoon wouldn't want those. Hey, you should do the talent show next year and add burnt fish sticks to the dartboard."

"Only if you do it with me. Think your mom would let you, as long as we didn't post it?"

"I don't see why not. We totally should."

"Sweet." And the cool thing is, I'm not worried that Mario will ditch me by then. We'll still be friends in a year. Probably much longer.

As I reach for my front doorknob, I hear a little growl.

"Uh, Jack?" Mario steps back. "To your left."

The raccoon has returned. He crouches beside the pillar, and I swear he flashes an evil grin before he stands up on his hind legs and hisses.

Gotta run!

Acknowledgments

This book is the result of many hands working together. Thanks to Chelsea Eberly and Diane Landolf, who helped edit the novel. To Amber Caraveo, my rock-star agent. To the illustrator, Billy Yong, who captured Jack's personality so brilliantly. To the entire team at Random House: the marketing team, designer Bob Bianchini, production manager Shameiza Ally, and copyeditors Barbara Bakowski and Janet Frick.

Finally, to my husband, Kevin, who helps me brainstorm and listens to me read my drafts, and to Mom, for her endless moral support.

When Ben accidentally becomes the
middle school mascot, Steve the Spud,
he isn't so sure he wants spec-**taters**. . . .

Turn the page NOW
for a sneak peek!

1
The Curse of the Potato

I don't know what I did to deserve it, but the fact is clear:
I, Ben Hardy, am cursed by potatoes. That demon veggie
has been out to get me for years.

Evidence #1: When I was five, I tripped over a bag
of potatoes and broke my arm. I had to wear an itchy
green cast for six weeks.

Evidence #2: My mom makes the world's gluey-est
mashed potatoes. They're great for craft projects.
Not for eating.

Evidence #3: There's a faded scar above my left
eyebrow. What happened? Let's just say I got on the
bad side of a cat named Tater Tot.

Then, two weeks ago, right in the middle of seventh grade, my family moved from Los Angeles to South Fork, Idaho—aka "the Potato Capital of the World." The people here worship the veggie like my dad worships the Lakers.

Case in point: my new school's game-day shirt. Today about half the school showed up wearing one. When I reach the cafeteria for lunch, I realize my friend Ellie is part of that half.

"You have to get one, Ben. Where's your school spirit?" Ellie plunks her lunch tray down and tosses her long black braid over her shoulder. On her shirt, a cartoon potato flexes its bulky biceps and flashes the kind of smile that should be reserved for clowns in horror movies.

Out of all the mascot options—the Cougars, the Eagles, the Saber-Toothed Tigers—my new school just *had* to be the Spuds. This crosses a line. At my last school, we were the Wildcats, ferocious and intimidating. All a potato can scare is . . . well, me, I guess.

I shake my head. "No way am I spending twenty bucks on that shirt. I could buy ten extra-large Slurpees for that price."

"What about Slurpees?" Our friend Hunter pulls off his hoodie as he sits at our table. He's wearing the shirt too. Somehow these two are totally oblivious to the uncoolness of waltzing around with a potato on your chest.

Ellie looks at Hunter. "No Slurpees. I'm just trying to get Ben to buy the game-day shirt. You're going with us tonight, right?"

"Can't," he says. "I'm still on foal watch." Hunter's horse Misty is super pregnant, so he and his dad have to sleep outside her stable in case she goes into labor. This is the kind of stuff people do in South Fork, Idaho.

Moving to a small town has been, to use Mom's words, "a bit of a culture shock." On the bright side, South Fork has less traffic and less smog. But then, there's no beach. No In-N-Out Burger. No skate park. On my first day, I showed up to school with a new haircut that would've been totally normal back in LA—short on the sides and swoopy on top. Too bad no one here has that haircut. I might as well have dyed my hair purple, I stick out so much.

Ellie shrugs at me. "Guess it's just us tonight. At least wear red."

I chug the rest of my chocolate milk. "Deal." Here's the best part about Idaho: Hunter and Ellie. Back in California, I didn't have anyone I could just go to basketball games with. My best friend moved to Canada at the beginning of the school year, so I ended up with a handful of sorta friends, but not a lot of hang-out friends. Sorta friends are the people you talk with about homework or mean teachers. Hang-out friends are the people you share food with or walk home with after school.

Hunter and I became friends when he offered me some Cheetos in science class on my first day. I helped him with his worksheet in return. The next day, he invited me to sit with him and Ellie in the cafeteria, which I appreciated, since, let's face it, the worst part of being the new kid is wondering who you'll eat with at lunch.

Sitting with Hunter and Ellie felt comfortable, like switching into sweatpants after school. They're the kind of people you can crack up with over dumb stuff, like Hunter's horrible Chewbacca impression or pictures of Ellie's poodle wearing socks. Last week, Ellie and I realized we live on the same street, so we've started walking home together. It makes trudging through the January weather a lot more bearable.

"Agh!" Hunter peers into his lunch sack, and his eyes bug out of his head. "Look what my mom packed me. A Go-Gurt and a can of tuna! With a can opener and everything! I can't eat this in public!"

"Then learn to make your own lunch," Ellie says.

"Learn to make your own face," says Hunter.

"That doesn't even make sense," says Ellie. She holds out half a sandwich. "Here, take this. I don't really like avocado anyway."

"What?" Hunter's face falls. "How can you not like avocado?"

She wrinkles her nose. "I think it's the texture."

"But . . . guacamole!"

"Just accept the sandwich!"

I try to stay out of these Ellie-and-Hunter arguments. They bicker like two people who've been stuck in the back seat of a car for nine hours. At first I thought it was because they were flirting, but—plot twist—they're just cousins. It's not obvious they're related. Hunter takes after the blue-eyed, pale-skinned white side of the family. Ellie has her Latina mom's brown eyes and complexion. If you look close enough, though, you'll notice the matching freckles across their noses.

I'm about to offer Hunter my string cheese when he jumps out of his seat and points under the table next to us. "Hot dog!"

Ellie buries her face in her hands. "Not again."

Hunter's obsessed with Chuck the Hot Dog, a game that's been popular at South Fork Middle School since the beginning of time, apparently. The cafeteria hot dogs are so rubbery that no one wants to eat them. They're more like pink erasers than meat. You can usually find them lying under tables or kicked into corners. Naturally, a game has sprung up where people throw them to see who can get the most bounces. (When no teachers are watching, of course.) Legend has it someone got twelve bounces once. Hunter says he's never gotten more than three or four.

Hunter ducks under the bench and crawls through a mob of knees. There's no time for dignity when a hot dog is involved. A minute later he reemerges, hot dog in hand. His proud face reminds me of the one Buster—my corgi—makes when we play fetch. They even have the same shaggy blond hair.

"Your turn." Hunter places the hot dog in my hand, and it's perfect. No squishes. No tears. Everything needed for optimum bounce-age.

But I don't want detention. Last week, Hunter got his "final warning" from the cafeteria monitor. Since we're friends, this "final warning" probably extends to me. I scan the room, fully expecting to see the monitor marching toward us with her stern expression. Luckily, it looks like she stepped out of the room.

"Hey, Ben's gonna chuck the hot dog!" A basketball player from two tables over points at me, and his teammates cheer me on. I had no idea that guy knew my name.

"You do it." I shove the hot dog back at Hunter, but he dodges.

"No, dude, you. It's his turn, right, Ellie?"

She lifts her palms up. "Leave me out of it. I'd rather you chuck it in the trash."

The basketball table stares at us, expecting a show, and all I can do is sit dumbly with the hot dog glued to my palm. They probably think I'm such a Goody Two-shoes. I want to throw it, but it's just not . . . *me*. I get in trouble for reading ahead during English. Not for throwing food.

A chant starts up at the basketball table. *Chuck it! Chuck it!* My cheeks burn up under the imaginary spotlight. There's no way I can do this. I've never gotten detention in my life.

But these guys don't know that. They don't know anything about me.

They *do* know my name, though. And something about that feels strangely good.

I squeeze the hot dog and slowly stand, my heart thumping to the beat of the chant.

Chuck it! Chuck it!

California Ben wouldn't dare.

Chuck it! Chuck it!

But nobody ever noticed him.

Chuck it! Chuck it!

Sometimes, change is good.

In the far corner of the cafeteria, the lunchroom monitor, Ms. Jones, reenters the cafeteria. She leans against the wall and swipes through her phone. I'll have to be quick.

I draw back my arm, aim for the clock, and throw as hard as I can. The hot dog zips through the air, smooth as a jet, and *boing*s off the 12, leaving a splotch of grease. Then it nose-dives for the vending machine, ricochets off the side, and tumbles halfway across the cafeteria like a rabid bunny.

Hunter and I cheer, along with the basketball crew. The athletes pump their fists in my honor, and I can't wipe the cheesy grin off my face.

Note to self: Chucking hot dogs is a great way to impress people.

I check to make sure Ms. Jones didn't see what just went down. Somehow she's still glued to her phone, totally oblivious to the lunchroom chaos. Thank goodness for technology.

Hunter smacks my back as I sit down. "Dude, you got six bounces! That's the most I've ever seen!"

Ellie tries to look annoyed, but her dimples betray her. "I know what I'm getting you guys next Christmas. A pack of jumbo hot dogs."

BLERRRRRRRP!

My body jolts as an air horn blasts through the cafeteria. The cheer squad jogs through the double doors at the far end of the room.

The tallest cheerleader holds a megaphone to her lips. "Heeeeey, South Fork Middle School!" Behind her, the girls shake their shiny red pom-poms.

Hunter points to Jayla, a blond cheerleader in the back row. He leans in. "There's your girl."

Fact check: Jayla's not my girl. She's way out of my league. Last week in English, I tossed a crumpled-up paper into the wastebasket and she said, "Nice shot." That's the extent of our relationship. I have no clue why Hunter has started teasing me about her.

Jayla does a high kick and lines up with her team. Her sleek ponytail flows halfway down her back like a golden waterfall. It looks so soft. And shiny. And—

Jayla catches my eye and I snap my head toward Hunter. He snorts and gives me a knowing grin. How embarrassing.

"All right!" the cheer captain yells into the megaphone. "I know you're all pumped for the BIG GAME TONIGHT!" The room erupts with applause.

"And what better way to spend your Friday night," she shouts, "than cheering on our South Fork Spuds against the Hamilton *Jackrabbits*." She sneers the word "Jackrabbits," and the students roar back with boos. Hamilton is our school's rival. From what I've heard, their reputation is definitely deserved. Once, they scattered rabbit poop across our team's locker room. These guys are bad news.

The head cheerleader sweeps her arm toward the doorway. "And now let's give a warm welcome to our very own Steeeve the Spuuud!"

I do a facepalm. "You've got to be kidding me."

A kid in a plushy potato costume bursts through the double doors. Weak cheers and snickers fill the cafeteria. The Spud mascot hops around and pumps his twiggy arms in the air like a giant beanbag come to life. He looks like Mr. Potato Head's nephew: the same cartoonish smile and googly eyes, but no mustache. Too bad. A mustache would significantly increase his coolness factor.

"Why do I go to a school that worships my least favorite vegetable?" I say.

Ellie nudges me. "Our school founders were potato farmers. Show some respect."

Music blares from the speakers, and Steve the Spud skips down the aisles, passing out high fives like he's some kind of celebrity. A few kids slap his hand, but most shrink away like he's got a contagious disease. This whole scene is so cringeworthy. Why would anyone in their right mind agree to wear that costume?

Suddenly the mascot's foot lands on the hot dog I flung across the cafeteria. His arms flail as the hot dog rolls under his foot. He shrieks and wobbles, trying to catch his balance, and—*splat!*— flops to the floor like a pancake.

THE TRAGIC FALL OF STEVE THE SPUD!

SLIP!

This is one of those moments where you're not supposed to laugh, but it's too funny to hold in. I mean, a potato flailing its arms, and the high-pitched scream . . . it's just too much. Hunter and I double over in laughter, along with most of the cafeteria. My hot dog—*my* hot dog—brought down the demon veggie. Today is definitely my day.

Ellie frowns. "Poor Wyatt. I hope he's not hurt."

I force myself to stop laughing. I guess I forgot there was an actual person inside that suit. "You know him?"

"Yeah, he sits by me in math."

That explains why I haven't heard of him. Ellie's a year ahead in math, so this Wyatt guy must be an eighth grader.

"I'm gonna go see how he's doing," Ellie says. She tucks her book under her arm and rushes over to Wyatt. On the other side of the cafeteria, a couple of teachers help him to his feet. It looks like he's okay. I hope so, anyway.

When the bell rings, I stand to go to English. My classroom is at the other end of the building, so I need to leave right now. I almost got a tardy yesterday. I toss my lunch into the trash bin at the end of the table. "See ya, Hunter."

"Not so fast, Mr. Hardy."

The voice comes from behind me. I whirl around and stare into the eyes of the lunchroom monitor, Ms. Jones, who is pinching a napkin-wrapped hot dog between her fingers.

YEARLING

Turning children into readers for more than fifty years.

**Classic and award-winning literature for every shelf.
How many have you checked out?**

**Find the perfect book and meet your
favorite authors at RHCBooks.com!**